Tasma Walton was born and raised in Western Australia and now lives in Melbourne. Since studying at NIDA, she has worked extensively as an actor on Australian television in series such as 'Blue Heelers', 'The Secret Life of Us' and 'City Homicide'. As a scriptwriter, she has several screenplays and a television series in development and she is also an accomplished artist. *Heartless* is her first novel.

heartless
TASMA WALTON

UQP

First published 2009 by University of Queensland Press
PO Box 6042, St Lucia, Queensland 4067 Australia
Reprinted 2009

www.uqp.com.au

© Tasma Walton 2009

This book is copyright. Except for private study, research, criticism or reviews, as permitted under the Copyright Act, no part of this book may be reproduced, stored in a retrieval system, or transmitted in any form or by any means without prior written permission. Enquiries should be made to the publisher.

Typeset in 12.5/16 pt Granjon Roman by Post Pre-press Group, Brisbane
Printed in Australia by McPherson's Printing Group

Cataloguing-in-Publication Data
National Library of Australia

Walton, Tasma, 1973–
Heartless / Tasma Walton.

ISBN 978 0 7022 3732 4

A823.4

University of Queensland Press uses papers that are natural, renewable and recyclable products made from wood grown in sustainable forests. The logging and manufacturing processes conform to the environmental regulations of the country of origin.

For Rove

prologue

I CANNOT FEEL MY heart beat.

Flashes of fluorescent light spike through my eyes and fire my mind. Sounds, pictures, scenes swim past in a haze, beckoning me to follow. I see myself clapping in a dusty auditorium in the middle of a row of proud, smiling faces. I see a dancing line of diminutive arms and legs, with sequins and wings and shining eyes. I think I see a familiar little face but it is impossible to grasp as the images form, then fragment instantly.

A door slams. I am jolted into another realm of wailing sirens, squeaking metal, barking voices and pinpricks against my skin. I know something is terribly wrong – the air is heavy and urgent with desperate action. I try to stay awake, to help, to understand the rushing around me, but I am called seductively back to those fragments sliding with the light through another part of my mind.

A glass door with my name on it swings open and a stylish hive of beige and burgundy cubicles stretches out before me. Very busy people buzz in and out. I know they are doing what I asked of them but I have no idea what that was.

The mirage dissipates and another rises in its place. The sound of a glass smashing on the wall behind me. Fierce eyes bulge at me, raging with anger and irrationality. I know this broken man, and I know this was not the only time his wounded fury burnt us both.

A lid is pushed off a green-and-white-striped shoe box. Treasures glitter inside, a turquoise pendant, a scruffy teddy bear, an even smaller box tucked away in the corner. I reach in to open it, but the shoe box falls out of my hands and into an abyss.

Another man's face takes sharp focus. Younger, softer, with a gentle voice and a resonant touch. I feel strongly that I want this scene to stay, to become the one I return to if my heart decides to beat again, but I am not sure why. He carries something precious in his hands and holds it out to me as a gift. Whatever it is radiates such a bright light that I have to shade my eyes for a moment and when I look back, he is gone.

Prologue

A strange painting shimmers into existence. Of a luminous white figure hovering in the air. She is surrounded by a golden wheel of light beams that radiate from a love heart in the centre of her chest. Her brightness pulses and blinds and becomes my mother's face.

My mum, white-faced and nose running, sits on her bed holding a pair of hair-cutting scissors. She shudders occasionally with the sobs of a cruel emotional catharsis. She looks at me with such deep disappointment that I feel sick to my stomach and the nausea rises leaden to my shoulders. Mercifully, the image fades, but the shame remains and I feel it seep into every cell in my body.

But I still cannot feel my heart beat. And an insistent thought hammers in my mind, saying that maybe, after everything I sense has happened, it would have been easier if I never had one. If I had been heartless.

Another flash of light stuns my eyes. Then suddenly, crisp and clear and compelling, I see myself at seven.

seven

I have a big, loud, red, dancing heart.

Adults, when they see her, say she is beautiful. They say she has so much joy and life pumping through, she might burst open at any moment and shower sparkles of brightness everywhere. When I show her to Mum and Dad, their eyes light up and they smile proudly. Dad says that I could do anything with such a happy and heavenly heart. Mum tells me if I always look after her and keep her shining like she does now, I will never take a wrong path.

My heart and I have many, long conversations. When my heart is excited, she beats really fast and loud like a rock song. At times like that, it can be very hard for me to get a word in edgewise, so I just sit back and listen. I take notes, in my all-time favourite pink-with-purple-dots-coloured diary, of all her grandest plans. Most of them revolve around playing and having as much fun as possible. Some of them take me away in my mind on terrific adventures. But my heart's favourite plan of all is for when we grow up. We will travel the world and find ourselves special, secret places, she says. And there we will uncover all the brilliant mysteries of life and write them down as magnificent stories and send them out to everyone on the planet. And as soon as the stories we write find people to read them, we will watch as their hearts start jumping for joy and their bodies start dancing in the street and their spirits start soaring freely upwards. My heart and I agree that this is our Great Life Purpose.

Until then, my heart wants us to practise getting shipwrecked on the beach. A truly horrible storm has torn our ship to pieces and thrown all living things into the rabid dog-barking ocean. My best friend Astintina and I get thrown a kilometre from our positions on the mast and are tossed and turned and thrashed nearly to death by the humungous waves. It must have looked quite convincing from the shore because Mum wades into the knee-high water to check that I am not having some sort of fit. Gasping weakly for air, I tell her that, by hook or by crook, we will make it to those distant shimmering

Seven

islands by nightfall. Mum suggests I should try and make it by lunchtime, otherwise she will be forced to eat my polony and sauce sandwiches on white bread, with Nana's lamingtons for dessert, all by herself.

*

It seems as though only my heart and I have the ability to see Astintina. It would be terribly lame to describe her as just a fairy. While she sparkles and shimmers and leaves showers of golden light as she moves, like a fairy does, she strongly dislikes mindless flitting and disappearing in puffs of glittery clouds. While her slim and slender, white, glowing body is only the size of a standard ruler, the glimmering mists of her energy can rise up and fill the biggest room. And Astintina refuses to wear wings of any description. She once thought of designing herself a very special cape of pure streaming sunlight but, in the end, discovered the art of sewing was not her particular gift. With all that said about not being a fairy, Astintina would never refuse an offer of fairy bread, definitely believes in fairy godmothers, loves town trees dressed in fairy lights, lists fairy penguins among her favourite animals and certainly appreciates an imaginative and well-told fairytale.

Heartless

My favourite thing about Astintina is her heart of light. Sometimes, she is so light-hearted, it lifts us all up and we have to sing and dance with the hairbrush in the mirror. Sometimes, when those angry, hissing words snake down the passageway from Mum and Dad's bedroom late at night, I feel my heart getting heavy with worry. In a split second, Astintina shines the light of her heart onto mine and the weight lifts off my chest and my heart remembers how free and perfect it is and so, floats like a fluffy cloud. And sometimes, in the dead-dark middle of night, when I wake up suddenly scared for no reason at all, my heart will leap into my mouth, hiding there, sending a pounding beat through my ears. Only Astintina can calm my heart down then. The light of her heart is a lantern in the deep dark, showing us the path to all the wonderful stories that are waiting in the black, waiting to be told when our Great Life Purpose as a writer begins.

*

Wednesday is the evening of our Glamour Dance Spectacular by Blossom's. We have been working for nearly a hundred decades on what Miss Blossom calls our piece de resistance, *The Magical Wonderland Ride with Alice and Her Mysterious Imaginings*. Due

Seven

to Kylie Robertson (everyone calls her Rabbits-on because of her unavoidable buck teeth and boring-to-death dribble) being chosen as a sympathy vote Alice, I am Mysterious Imagining Number Seven.

After a quick consultation with my heart, we decide the only possible way of making this remotely fun is to dress as Astintina. She agrees, and helps me with an intricate, cutting-edge, finger-painted design. On a brilliant gold background, we carefully paint her flowing form in bright white, resisting the temptation to add feet, because Astintina insists that under her dress she does not have, and never has had, legs, knees, ankles, feet or toes. Thankfully, she does make a concession with the arms. While Astintina moves armless, gracefully arching her body from side to side, I explain Miss Blossom's choreography involves whole minutes of waving arms above the head making letters, walking like an Egyptian queen might, and random combinations of swimming strokes. So the arms have to remain, but we decide they should be painted white to maintain some real-life resemblance.

For a long while, we puzzle over how to show the streaming beams of light that forever shine from Astintina's heart. Quite accidentally, as I rehearse with absolute focus on Miss Blossom's overarm into breaststroke into dolphin diving dance routine, I knock over my falling-apart bicycle and the front wheel rolls off. As it lies on the floor, spinning wonkily, Astintina throws a penny from the heavens into my head and my heart manages to catch it as it drops out a fully fledged idea. Look to the wheel, is the thought. So I do and it suddenly makes sense. The circular, pointing-out pattern of the wheel spokes looks like the nearly perfect way to show Astintina's beams of light. To avoid any eye poking mishaps, we decide it would be best to cover the spokes in soft, gold material and make them bigger and longer with stuck-together straws, until they become an almost classified-by-science sun, streaming out from behind my back.

Finally, one crowning touch is the only thing needed to complete our design masterpiece. For such important matters, gold foil is the only choice, in the shape of the world-renowned love heart, and taking pride of place in the centre of the chest, Astintina's beautiful, light, golden heart.

Mum spent a good couple of hours sewing my Mysterious Imagining Number Seven outfit, the Glowing Fairy. Even though we all strongly disliked the name, I thought it easier not to try and explain to Mum about it being a tribute to Astintina. While it is a design sensation, the wheel spoke sun of light beams is definitely the most challenging

Seven

bit, not just for Mum to have sewn, but also for me to wear. Kids who never look where they are going continuously bashed into it during our final dress rehearsal, so I have been extra careful not to go near anyone since.

At last, the time has come. Kylie Rabbits-on, tonight known as Alice, has just started her welcome speech, I have just gulped down two cups of strawberry crush cordial, and, as I realise there is no way they will let me go to the toilet now, my heart starts to panic and flutter. Flapping around like a freaked-out butterfly in an unfriendly rib cage, making me feel horribly sick in my stomach, my heart needs a whole thirteen breaths, quietly counted in by Astintina, to calm her down. The next minute, Miss Blossom gives me an almighty push and I trip embarrassingly, not at all walking like the Egyptian queen I am meant to be, onto the stage.

Caught unawares by the blinding lights, my heart goes nuts again, leaping into my mouth and sending her frantic beat through my ears, almost completely drowning out the music. Luckily, I see Mysterious Imagining Number Five – nobody knows what happened to Number Six – at the end of the letter 'L' and so I launch into the 'O' position and accompanying wiggle routine. I blur through the 'V', shout out the 'E', because Miss Blossom decided there was not really a way to do it properly with your arms, and only start to enjoy the whole experience when we get to the swimming strokes.

It is after the overarm and going into the breaststroke that I see Mum in the middle of the fourth row. She is laughing and clapping and gives me a wave. I wave back as I do my dolphin dives, one in the middle, one to the left and one to the right, scanning the audience for Dad. I hold my nose for the finishing move, wish wash wiggle down to the floor, try not to break my wheel spoke light beams, then throw my arms out wide as the music comes to an end. Everyone jumps up from their seats clapping, some smiling, some frowning, some laughing, some crying. Mum waves to me again. There is no sign of Dad.

*

Hospital smell would have to be one of the worst smells in the world, right up there with egg farts and vomit. Sick people and medicine and cleaning products all gang up to try and make every visiting well person feel like they should be in a hospital gown too. My heart goes really quiet in the hospital, sad for the people she senses are dying. And nobody really feels like playing, having fun, laughing or even smiling in this place. I know Mum hates the

Seven

idea of having to stay overnight. I can see that her heart has tightened into a little ball and is trying to hide in the folds of her left lung. Unfortunately, it still cannot stop itself from going into a funny little shaking spasm from time to time. A heart flutter, the doctors say. Mum will have to stay and survive the smell through a long night, so her heart can be watched and monitored and documented. Astintina thinks Mum's heart has forgotten how to jump for joy and the spasms are desperate attempts at trying to remember. I think Mum's heart is scared of something but I am not sure exactly what.

Dad cooks me slightly soggy fish fingers with milky mash and mint-sauced peas. We do the dishes together and afterwards I use the tea towel as the red rag in my new bull-fighting dance routine Miss Blossom is teaching us. My heart loves it when Dad watches us dance. She shines like the brightest star in the night sky and gushes of warm love beat through her when he claps us at the end. He reads us half a bedtime fairytale and his character voices get the nod of approval from Astintina. When Dad tucks us in tight like snug bugs in a rug, my heart and I feel the safest ever. Even when the light is switched off and he walks away and the darkness starts to buzz, we easily drift off to sleep in a sea of fuzzy happiness.

Heartless

I was in the middle of a going to the toilet dream when I woke up just in time to stop myself from wetting the bed. There is almost no worse thing than having to stay awake long enough to pull myself out of bed, make it down the passageway without falling over and get to the toilet in time. I only just managed to do it with little more than a quarter of a minute to spare before I would have weed in my pyjamas.

Television sounds from the living room travel into the bathroom, gunshots and horses' hooves and yee-has. It is so late into the night I think that maybe the slow bits in the show have made Dad fall asleep and maybe now the action will wake him up. I go in to see, yawning with the biggest mouth possible, and only just manage to make it all the way to the living room standing upright. An old western movie is playing on the television. A strange lady with nearly no clothes on is sitting on our couch. Dad with nearly no clothes on is kissing her.

My heart freezes. My brain goes numb. My legs start shaking. But luckily, they are still able to carry me back to my bedroom without making the slightest noise. In bed, with the covers pulled right up over my whole body like a tent, I try to get my heart to start moving properly. She can only manage a shiver and it is making me feel quite dizzy in

Seven

the head. A scared, trembling thought keeps running round and round in my brain, thinking that my heart will never recover from this shock, that all her grandest plans will fade away and that our Great Life Purpose will never even start.

Astintina is doing her best, breathing with my heart, whispering 'it's all rights' and singing wordless lullabies. I join in with a small dry voice, humming and rocking with her gently in our body. Long and late into the night, with Astintina's heart of light weaving her magic, my cold little heart finally starts to thaw. Pump by pump, she remembers her rhythm and sets about spreading warmth around our body. Little by little, bit by bit, we come back to the life we know. Last of all, slowly warming, but still sad about life, my shocked little heart manages to send the tiniest of rivulets of blood to bring relief to my now freezing feet.

*

It has been most of May and a little bit of June since Mum came out of the hospital. She was given some pills and told to take it easy. All this time, both my heart and I have been waging a battle within ourselves about whether we should say what we saw. Usually we both know straightaway the best path to follow and go down it in perfect agreement. Climb the tree, yes. Play in the drain, no. Steal the chocolate, no. Ask Mum if we can buy it, yes. This is very different. We have made endless lists in our diary of all the reasons why we should tell and all the reasons why we should not. It has not helped one little bit to show us the way. And Astintina just smiles like a painting at us when we ask what she would do.

School holidays are almost over and Mum cuts my hair as usual. She always wanted to be a hairdresser and would have been terrifically successful, but gave birth to me instead. As the scissors snip like a lonely bird and I watch my hair fall like skinny feathers to the floor, my heart suddenly bursts with a massive beat and the words suddenly blurt out loudly from my mouth.

Are you allowed to kiss someone else besides Dad when you're married?

What do you mean, sweetie?

Would it be a bad thing for you to kiss someone else besides Dad?

The scissors stop snipping and Mum turns me around. Her face is pale and mine goes red. Her heart barely moves and mine is racing. She whispers the same question she asked before.

What do you mean, sweetie?

And I whisper back.

Seven

Daddy kissed someone on the couch when you were in hospital.

Then and there, Mum's heart leaps out of her chest with a jolt and drops like a dead weight to the floor. Stiff with shock, her fingers let the scissors slide from their grip. It seems so slow I should be able to catch them. But then it seems so fast I cannot think straight. The scissors stab straight through the middle of Mum's heart.

*

Her heart bled continuously for the next twenty-four hours. All the violent words that streamed from Mum's mouth during that time were desperately trying to make Dad's heart bleed too. Instead, his heart pounded with a vicious, righteous beat, whipping itself up into battle mode and wielding a metal shield in front of it to stop any knifed thoughts from stabbing it to bits. Mum's weakened, fluttering heart was no match for that. In the end, the poor frail thing almost bled itself dry. Lifeless, spent, no strong red colour remaining, just pale, defeated. Nothing left to protest with as Dad packed up his clothes and things into suitcases and boxes and made plans to leave us and never return.

All this time, my heart and I stayed huddled in our room. We had nothing to say to each other.

Slowly creeping over us was a sticky sludge of sickly fear saying it was all our fault. Saying we never should have said anything. Never, ever, should have said anything. And this fearful sludge would not be stopped, oozing all through my body, blocking up my ears, sniffling up my nose, clouding over my eyes and covering my heart in a shroud of shame. I write in my diary, we never should have said anything.

I could barely see Astintina through all that haze. Even though I knew she was shining her brightest, frantically moving, waving, sending out extra special laser beams of light to me, they all seemed to be covered in an army of the dullest lampshades. Her angelic silver streaming laugh, usually the most beautiful sound I ever did hear, could not even reach my clogged-up, deaf-with-fear ears. And worst of all, my heart had wrapped herself in a heavy cloak of sadness and turned her back to the world and so, did not even know that Astintina's brave heart was pulsing with all the electric joy it had, trying desperately to kick-start our nearly flat-lining life.

There was a knock at the door. Dad came in. His big angry heart was still pounding out its battle beat, pounding away any trace of sadness that might have threatened it.

I'll see you next weekend.

My heart flapped and fluttered.

Seven

Don't go, Daddy.
He turned to go.
Look at me, Daddy!
He turned back.

And my heart and I sprang into life. We danced for him. We danced for survival, for family, for love. We danced with every ounce of happiness and heaven we had. And as we danced, we knew we had never shined brighter than in that moment. We had never been more beautiful than in that moment. We had never before shown the deepest depths of our love, how much love we had to give and how much love we needed back, than in that moment.

In one swift move, Dad whisked us up and held us close. Three words whispered in my ear.

I love you.

My heart was in his hands. She was still dancing, beating in quick time, sparkling and shining. I was enfolded in his arms, still open and loving and hoping with all my might he would stay. Then he put me down. Turned his back. Walked away. My heart still in his hands, dancing in desperation.

Mum flew into a rage.

You heartless bastard!

Currents of fury and agony and fear swept through, drowning all the love in the room. Fists and curses and mean spirits pummelled to pieces all the life in the room. In the chaos, I saw Dad drop my heart to the floor and as she hit it with a resounding thud, she broke beyond repair. Then, as Dad struggled to get past Mum and out of the house, his boots crushed my heart to pieces. Then, as Mum raced to fling her parting shots at Dad, her shoes kicked my fractured heart into a damp and dusty corner.

And so, dirty and displaced in the dark lies my heart. Broken. Bruised. Bleeding. I kneel down to collect her and notice some pieces are missing. Probably stuck to Dad's boots. I find one smashed piece near the door, but my heart refuses to take it back. My heart refuses to even look at me. She was a big, loud, red, dancing heart. Now she is shattered, mute, blue, and numb with pain. I put her back into my chest.

*

Dad left town the following day on a plane flying interstate. He did not come back on the weekend to see me. He did not come back for three and a half months. When he did come back, he drove me to the beach and we built sandcastles and ate ice-cream and talked about Miss Blossom's dance class. It lasted just under two hours. Then he left on a plane for interstate again.

Seven

As soon as I hear a plane in the sky, I run as fast as I can into the backyard to see it. I jump up and down and wave as hard as I can because that could be the plane Dad is on. I make sure I keep jumping and waving while the plane turns into a tiny speck in the sky and I make sure I keep jumping and waving until it disappears completely. I know it would make Dad very upset if he was on that plane and saw our house and nobody was waving to him. And maybe, if Dad was on that plane and flew over our house and saw me jumping and waving, maybe that might make him remember us and want to come and live with us again.

*

I stole the steak knife from the second drawer in the kitchen one evening when Mum was in the shower. I keep it in my pillowcase for when I go to sleep at night. I would use it if I have to. Especially after I have that running-in-the-street nightmare. It is always the same. I am in my pyjamas. I am running down the middle of a very nice street being chased by something black and evil that wants to kill me. I am very upset and try to knock on the front doors of the lovely-looking houses in this pretty street, asking for someone to let me in so I am safe. I bash on the first front door, crying and calling out, but no one answers. I can see them sitting as a family having dinner and I know they can hear me but they do not want to open their door for me. The monster is getting closer, so I race to the next house. They shake their heads and will not let me in either. I get more and more scared as the monster gets closer and closer. But still, no one will let me in. No one will keep me safe. No one cares. As the monster is about to catch me, I wake up. I make sure my knife is still there and I hold it up to the darkness as a warning to anyone around that I would use it if I had to.

When I first got the knife, Astintina laughed at me and told me I was silly. I told her to go away. It is not the same anymore. No matter how much light Astintina tries to shower me with, it no longer makes any difference. The black of the night is enormous now and whirls around my room whispering bad things in my ear and creating bad thoughts in my head. It reminds me that I am all alone now and no dad will ever tuck me in snug as a bug again. It hisses that it could get me any time it wants because no dad will come and save me at the right moment; in fact, no dad will come at all. The light beams from Astintina's heart have no chance against a dark such as this, so I tell her that I am tired and things are different and I will not be listening anymore.

Seven

She refuses to go away, she adamantly spreads her light, she dances and laughs and shines, but I still ignore her.

Adults used to say my heart had so much joy and life pumping through, she might burst open at any moment and shower sparkles of brightness everywhere. Dad used to say that I could do anything with such a happy and heavenly heart. Mum used to tell me if I always looked after her and kept her shining, I would never take a wrong path. My heart no longer has any joy and life, certainly no showering sparkles of brightness. She is not happy, she is not heavenly and she is not shining. After the day Dad left, there was nothing I could do to look after her. I write in my diary that with my heart as it is now, I know deep down that I will not be able to do anything I dream of and that I will probably choose the wrong path without even knowing it.

Now, my heart sits still in my chest, broken and battered, with pieces missing and coloured blue. She bleeds too, sluggish seeping drops of blaming and being ashamed. We never should have said anything.

I prefer not to talk to my heart anymore and I try not to look at her either. She is ugly and I know that I am ugly too. There is no point in playing anymore and our grand plans for our Great Life

Heartless

Purpose were a silly idea anyway. I do not write interesting stories anymore. The only thing I write in my diary now is how I wish my heart would stop aching. Sometimes, she aches so much I start crying and crying and find it hard to stop. Sometimes, she aches so much I want to rip her out and throw her away. Sometimes, she aches so much I wish I never ever had a heart in the first place. Like what Mum said Dad was when he left us. Heartless.

fourteen

We had been kissing, along with other stuff, on the oval behind the netball courts for about twenty minutes and the lawn was making my back itchy. I was turned on, but not, like, hugely, mainly because my boyfriend had no idea where to find my clitoris. Probably did not even know such a thing existed. And I could not really be bothered giving him lessons or doing it myself after such a hard netball game, playing centre for three quarters and goal attack for the last and still not winning. I could hear people coming and going nearby but luckily we had found a secluded spot so I guess we were fairly safe.

We were doing the usual things. He sucked my boob, I rubbed his dick, he fingered me and a part of me was actually feeling quite bored. Really, all

I wanted to do was maybe just lay down and cuddle or something. My favourite thing has always been to just lay in their arms, smelling their male smell, touching their male skin and hearing the beat of their male heart. Talking while cuddling would be the all-time greatest score, but I was yet to meet a guy who enjoyed hugging more than making out and who could string more than three words together. Yeah, nup and whatever were pretty much it and if you got all three at once, the heavens shook.

This was the fourth time I had gotten it on with this guy, my boyfriend officially, according to the notes that were passed around and what his mates confirmed when they asked me out on his behalf. He was a year and a half older than me, reasonably cute, developing biceps, had surfie-style blonde hair and, quite literally, four darker hairs on his upper lip. His voice was doing that breaking thing which was actually quite funny but I never laughed at him because I know he got embarrassed and I felt sort of sorry for him.

I had only glimpsed his heart once, for the split-test of seconds, when he first put his hands in my pants. It was a closed-up tight little bud of a thing, mostly green, except in a moment of excitement when it would quickly flush red and pump spurts

Fourteen

of blood in a downward direction. From what I had learnt in my experiences, most boys had hearts like this. Not really open yet, not ready to flower yet, not ready to be revealed yet. Which is okay with me. My heart is a constricted little ball that hides behind my left lung, like my mum's does, with scars and discolourations, totally worn and unattractive. I do not intend showing anyone my heart in a hurry.

Surreptitiously, I glanced at my watch and knew Mum would be pulling into the car park to pick me up any moment now. Just as I was about to tell him I had to go, he looked at me red faced and breathless, pulled a condom from his jeans and asked me if I would do it with him. He was a virgin and so was I. He kissed me surprisingly tenderly. He held me close. He whispered in my ear he loved me. I saw his heart flush deep red for a beat. For the first time in a long time, my heart stirred into action and leapt to my throat, still weak but driven by panic, pounding a resounding no no no through my body. For seven years now we had barely spoken to each other and when we did we never really agreed on anything. Neither one of us trusted the other's judgment so what was the point of consultation. I took the condom.

Who would have thought it would hurt like hell

the first few times he pushed his dick inside me. No one prepares you for that. I nearly could have screamed. Luckily it was not long before he came. I did not even get remotely close, which was really okay because I was, more than anything, relieved it was over. The actual sex itself was sadly disappointing but I enjoyed the minute of holding each other afterwards. Then I looked at my watch and knew I had to hurry like quick sticks, get my knickers back on and get the hell out of there. I told him my mum was waiting for me and I had to go. He offered me a cigarette. I told him the least he could do was to give me a couple.

A plane flew overhead as I raced to where Mum was parked. I stopped and looked at it, resisted the urge to wave like I would when I was seven, felt my heart spasm and suddenly had to stop myself from crying.

*

After relentlessly nagging me about my room, my homework, my dirty dishes, my running late, my rudeness, my rolling eyes and my not brushing my teeth, Mum has finally gone to bed. I have been hanging out all afternoon and night to smoke one of the boyfriend's cigarettes. Quietly as I can, I sneak out to the backyard and light up. I breathe in, I breathe

Fourteen

out. In the black night, the buzzing silence, the cigarette smoke and the seeming peace, I think about the day.

I lost my virginity today. I write this in capital letters in my space themed, black with blue planets on it diary. My virginity, lost, gone, never to be found again. My vagina was sore when I washed it in the shower. I always thought I would feel different when it happened, important, special, a woman. But I feel a little bit empty, a little bit sad about it. A little bit like I wished it had happened in a whole other way. But the power in those three words. He told me he loved me. I have not heard those words from a male's mouth since I was seven and I think I went into shock, even though, deep down, I knew it was a lie. Maybe not a conscious lie, but I had seen his heart and knew that it was nowhere near capable of understanding, let alone feeling, the sort of love he was inferring.

Of course, my heart pipes up with a timid I told you so and I have to remind her that even she flushed a little when he said I love you. Regardless of her protestations, to hear those words was quietly wonderful. Even my nagging heart has to admit, as stupid as it sounds, those three little words sparked a nice and certainly welcome warm rush through my body and maybe that was enough for him to deserve my virginity as a reward. Maybe those words were just what I needed to hear after so long. I tell my heart and write in my diary, what does it matter now anyway. My heart shuts up.

The end of my cigarette crackles and burns. Sometimes, little shoots of light fly off it into the dark. Quite randomly, I think of Astintina. A welcome relief, changing the subject. I cannot remember the last time I thought of that crazy little imaginary friend, who looked suspiciously like a fairy but insisted there were key differences in her appearance that had to be taken into account. Really, I was a freak of a seven-year-old. I wonder where Mum put that finger painting I did of her. The outrageous design of that ridiculous costume for Miss Blossom's Dance Shit-acular. Four long years with that bitch-face cow was enough to send any girl insane. No wonder I was caught playing kiss chasey with Fuddly Dudley near the toilets when I was eleven and got kicked out of the class; I was bored out of my bloody brain. I stamp out my cigarette.

Back inside, I turn the laundry light on and partially close the door. When I crawl into bed I make sure I can still see a patch of light on the floor in my bedroom from the laundry. I double-check the steak knife is in easy reach inside my pillowcase. I turn on my side, facing the light, to sleep. And slowly, as

Fourteen

always, I feel it creep through my chest. That ever-present ache of my heart. She says she cannot help it and I just have to learn to live with it. Sometimes, on a relatively normal day, her aches are dull and only mildly annoying. But sometimes, after a day like today, her aches throb and burn and bring tears to my eyes and before I know it, my throat is constricting, my shoulders grow heavy, my body shudders and I am crying. I hate it, the sobbing, the snot, the stooped-up crying. I cannot stop it and I hate it.

*

Sitting on a Greyhound bus full of breathing, sneezing, coughing, talking, laughing, snorting, scaly people for nine miserable hours is a slow, insidious, bum-numbing torture designed to completely mess with a girl's head. One measly cigarette break goes nowhere in restoring a modicum of mild sanity. I suck down the smoke of three cigarettes in a row whilst hiding behind the semitrailer parked near the toilet, away from the disapproving glares of the Respectable Young Ladies with their tucked-in white blouses and tailored, grey skirts. Finally, the bus arrives at our interstate, small-town destination and I see Dad has brought along his whole new, ever-smiling family brood to welcome me. Herald the joyful choir of angels. Not.

Playing stepmother is the strange lady with nearly no clothes on who was sitting on our couch kissing Dad. My fellow step-family members include a six-year-old boy – they wasted no time – who kicks lamp poles and street signs and his sister when no one is looking. A four-year-old, the often-kicked sister who can scream and cry with the best of them, but does not seem to know how to just talk normally. And a chubby, gurgling, clapping nine month old who plays the chirping cherub during the day and the screeching banshee at night.

Then there is my dad. I travel to stay at his new house every other school holidays for just under a week. I see him on random weekends, once every couple of months, always with his new family in tow. My mum and dad barely talk to each other face to face, preferring to use those deathly boring 'tell your father he'd betters' and 'let your mother know thats'. Of course, I am the messenger and, more often than not, get shot. It has been nearly seven years since I spent time with my dad alone. Probably for the best because I figure we would not know what to say to each other if we did.

Before we head back to their house, Dad wants to get a photo on the cliffs overlooking the main beach. It happens every time I arrive, an old routine and after the arduous bus trip and the not-really-

Fourteen

welcome welcoming party, it is a miracle this acutely annoying habit does not drive me completely over the edge. In fact, to my continuous surprise and amazement, each time the photos are eventually developed, I always seem to have managed to pull an incredibly convincing happy face.

This time they want me to hold the baby. Curiously, it does not cry once the whole time it is in my arms. As all the fuss is made over who stands where, I look at the bundle in my arms. It looks straight back at me and smiles. And then I see its tiny perfect precious heart steadily beating a simple song. Gently red like a freshly picked golden delicious apple, it knows of all things good and happy and safe. As I gaze at this clean, new heart, I know that it is truly lovely and sweet and bright. I know that it is wonderfully pure and innocent and nice. And I know I cannot stand to keep looking at it. So I look down instead to the waves crashing violently on the rocks below. They rumble and churn, wild and fierce and very hungry. They call out to my envious piecemeal heart.

Throw the little one to us! Go on, you stumble, the baby falls. Easy!

I look to the baby's unsuspecting heart as the flash from the camera blows my fantasy away.

Two days later, the photos are developed. Only I

can see the truth behind that sinister smile plastered on my face.

*

Nothing really special happens on these holidays. Much of the time is spent getting kids ready, doing dishes, going to the playground and swimming at the safe end of the town pool. Sometimes, Dad will play cricket with me on the median strip, which is great until the stepbrother runs off with the ball like a yappy little Shih tzu, desperate to steal all the attention, and I have to make sure he is safe from oncoming traffic while Dad tries to get the ball back.

Sometimes, we will all go to the park for a family picnic and while Dad is setting up the spread and stepmother juggles wiping snot from the baby and the stepsister's respective noses, I climb up a grand old Moreton Bay fig. I imagine I am in my very own dream tree house, watching out for pirates and gremlins and marauding armies. Next thing I know, I am relegated to an even lower rung on the social pariah ladder, because stepbrother has tried to follow me, has fallen off and has given himself a gushing great nosebleed. Only my diary provides a sanctuary.

In the evenings, the bath times are strictly regulated. Stepmother always has a shower first, then

Fourteen

runs the bath for the kids. I help her out, washing their hair and playing rinse-off with the squidgy fish that squirts water from its mouth. I really am very careful not to let anything get in the children's eyes. Really. Then it is my turn to take my two-minute-only shower, otherwise there is no water left for Dad and the baby. They shower together. Through the tiniest crack in the study door, where my mattress has been set up on the floor, I can see their outlines in the shower. I watch as the silhouette of Dad holds the baby up to the showerhead and I hear the baby squeal with delight. I listen as Dad ums and ahs to the baby, calling her his precious little girl, his little ray of sunshine, his sweetest little pea, his all-time favourite. Then I quietly close the study door as the shower turns off and their playtime is over and I sit with my arms wrapped around my chest trying to stop the stabbing sensations in my jealous heart.

On the weekend, after the mandatory viewing of the local footy match where I get lucky and pass the time by pashing an older guy with the colours of the opposition on, a boisterous group of Dad and Stepmother's mates come back to the house for a barbecue. During the passage of beer, sausages, meringue and hours, I am reintroduced with jovial rounds of 'you remembers' and 'haven't you grown's'. Throughout the evening I wander around with at least three pairs of eyes on me at all times, which quickly glance away when I gather the courage to look back. Every now and then, caught on the conspiring breeze, I hear the sharp whisperings of 'a previous marriages', 'doesn't look like hims' and 'not much spark about hers'.

Empty, quiet, dark, I blissfully hide in the living room. I curl up on the couch in the corner to catch my breath and let the red drain from my cheeks. Women's voices enter the kitchen.

It must be over six months.
Must be.
She's certainly filled out.
Someone needs to get her on a diet.
Don't really see her father in her.
Her mother's dark, apparently.
That explains it.
He must've been young when they married.
She got pregnant apparently.
Only twenty-two, he was.
Oh well, no wonder he left.
It's great that he lets her come and stay for holidays.
Must be hard on the other kids.
Well she's a bit of a moody little thing, isn't she?
Bit of a sourpuss if you ask me.
No wonder the other kids don't seem to like her.

Fourteen

Haven't seen her smile once.
Not at all like her father.

The voices fade out and the kitchen door swings shut. The red has flooded back into my cheeks. My humiliated heart hangs her head in shame. And I just want to punch a hole in the salmon-pink wall, rip the entire reputable place apart, scream out the rage in my lungs, then crawl under a rock and die.

*

On my last night at Dad's house, I have that stupid nightmare again. It seems so pathetic in the morning when I think about it, but in the middle of the dark night, the pressing black, when my senses are wired and my fear is wrought, it is very real and horrible. Quite simply, in the nightmare, I am a tiny thing in a massive room. That is all it is. I am huddled up, terrified, in the corner of a sickeningly towering room. Looking up at the gigantic walls, I get dizzy with a nauseating wave of vertigo. The colossal room seems to tilt and spin and the swarming size of it threatens to crash upon me, engulf me, decimate me, obliterate me.

Worst of all, when I wake up feeling strangulated with fear, blackness all around, the nightmare travels with me into reality. I struggle to get my bearings in the space and the darkness seems immense, laden with ill will, crushing down upon me. Trying desperately to centre my spinning body without throwing up, I fumble for the steak knife in my pillowcase. Only then, when I grasp it firmly in my two hands and hold it up against the pummelling dark, do I feel reality settle back into place. With the blade as a starting point, a warning, the dimensions of the room begin to restructure and return to normal. I am no longer tiny, huddled in the corner, but stretched out on my mattress, larger, filling the space, claiming it. Even so, I do not want to go back to sleep again. I keep the knife clutched to my chest and stay awake on the mattress in my Dad's study until the first light of morning. Then, I creep out of bed and replace my stepmother's steak knife in her well-organised cutlery drawer, write in my diary that I had the dream again and pack my bag to leave.

The best moment of all comes when Dad hugs me goodbye. For several seconds I am wrapped in his big strong arms, feeling his big strong heart beat steady and sure and a glimmer of warmth brushes my hidden away heart. She jumps for joy and almost makes me blurt out I love you to him. Thankfully, with all the eyes of the new family on me, I refrain from saying anything and Dad ends the hug.

But it is a moment I replay over and over, during

Fourteen

the long trudging nine hours back to Mum, in the bus loaded with too many people. I suspend it, elongate every nanosecond, heighten every tiny touch and stretch thick every warm sensation. I let myself ricochet back in time to my cherished flimsy memory of when I was the little baby and I was the one Dad held in the shower and I was bathed in his loving favouritism. I use it to flesh out those fleeting fragments of scenes I randomly remember: Dad lifting me over the waves, Dad carrying me out of the car, Dad raising me up to touch the ceiling, Dad pulling me down off the swing. For weeks after, I sit alone, close my eyes, wrap my arms around me and remember that moment.

Then, slowly, the memory fades.

*

It seems as though, as I have grown breasts, Mum has grown into a bitch-face cow. Constantly criticising what I wear, the way I walk, the words that come from my mouth, she even hates the way I think.

Where's your head young lady?

Trying hard to resist breaking into a full-grown smirk, I am greatly amused by the notion of my being a lady. If only she knew about my oval experience behind the netball courts, I swear she would internally combust on the spot.

Answer me!

What!?

I said where is your head!

Geez, Mum, on my friggin' neck.

Don't you talk to me like that! You know what I mean.

What am I doing wrong now!

Look at that dress you're wearing! You've got slabs of make-up on. You're all tarted up, people are talking. What d'you say about that?

Let them talk, I think. I hate people anyway.

Cat got your tongue, has it? What d'you say about that?

I hate them and I hate you!

And once again, Mum's delicate and defaced heart drips a little tear of blood.

Sometimes, when she hears those whispers in the shopping centre, she gets so worked up, she raves and rants like a madwoman off the street and has to take an extra heart tablet. Sometimes, she gets so disappointed in me, she leaves the house in a huff to walk it off for an hour. Sometimes, she gets so hopelessly frustrated, she only just manages to stop herself from whacking me with the wooden spoon.

Other times, Mum does not say anything at all. Just stares at me with a strange expression in her eyes. Like a cocktail of regret and blame, guilt

Fourteen

and fear, shame and defeat. Then, wordlessly, she will go to her room and close the door. It does not matter where I go in the house, it is impossible to escape the sound of her weeping. It tears through the walls, fills every available space and saturates all the atoms in the air. No matter how hard I try to cover myself in not caring, her pain penetrates every cell in my body. It seeks out the mirror image, compatriot pain I have carefully hidden in my heart and exposes it without a trace of tender mercy. My heart bleeds broken dams full of pent-up pain and I drown in the flood of it.

Eventually, I go to her door, red-eyed and heaving. I knock and she opens it, also red-eyed and heaving. She sits back down on the edge of her bed like a broken little bird fallen from the nest. Her face wears that lonely, lost expression it had in the first few weeks after Dad left us, and I feel my face form its reflection. We look at each other and see the same pain, the same sorrow, the same abandonment, the same sense of utter loneliness. We see each other's wounded hearts and hold each other close. I whisper, choking, in her ear.

I am sorry . . . for everything.

And she whispers back.

I am sorry for everything too.

*

Heartless

A week later I am grounded. I am not allowed to go to the concert with my new boyfriend. Not the guy from the oval behind the netball courts, I dropped him as a matter of course after the incident, but an even older guy who works as an apprentice something with his dad and lives four blocks away from me. It is particularly annoying because that is the night of an incredibly rare occurrence. The boyfriend's parents will be away for the weekend and have, for the first time in history, left him alone to look after the house without the presence of a responsible adult.

As the hours tick by, and Mum stays up doing the ironing, it becomes clear I am going to miss the concert. In disgust, I decide to go to bed early. And wait. It is another two and a half hours before Mum finally switches off the television, turns out the lights and starts snoring from her bedroom. With cunning calculation, I wait another thirty minutes before making my move. Like a highly skilled assassin, with cat burglar instincts and professional athlete prowess, I slide out of my bedroom window, creep down the side of the house, scale the two-metre-high back fence and walk low and quick to the corner of the street. From there, I sprint like a cheetah in its prime the four blocks to my boyfriend's house.

Fourteen

The house is deceptively quiet from the street and I fleetingly wonder if everyone is still at the concert. I tentatively go to the door and knock. No answer. My scared little heart flares up and demands to be taken home. She flaps, frightened, not feeling good about being here. I shush her and steady myself, I am here now after all. Taking a deep breath, I scale the gate leading into the backyard and make like Elmer Fudd hunting rabbits to the back door. It swings open. A seductive beat wafts past, laden with cigarette smoke, whiskey and another pungent, herbaceous odour I cannot name. The party is definitely on.

I find my new boyfriend, swaying but still comprehensible, holding court in the games room extension with a small group of three red-eyed, sweating, half-smirking, half-grimacing, partially clothed young adults. Another four have passed out at various points and in various positions around the room, one cradling for dear life an empty ice-cream container. A half-hearted cheer is raised when I wave a little hello and my boyfriend throws his arm around me, mainly to keep his balance, then loses it, faux crash tackling me down to the couch. A bottle of whiskey doing the rounds is circulated our way and I take my first ever swig of hard liquor. Feeling like it is burning a welt down the inside of my throat, I quickly throw back the glass of water from the coffee table in front of me. Very bad move. Judging by the now raging inferno in my throat and the jeering applause from the group, that was not water in the glass.

Half an hour and three swigs later, I am starting to lose my ability to focus and the room is starting to spin at the edges. Two others have passed out and I am feeling like I should do the same. My boyfriend is taking my top off which I am slightly uncomfortable about because his friend in the corner keeps staring at us. My boyfriend reassures me it is okay and that his friend has seen it all before and that I can keep my bra on if it makes me feel better. The friend is rolling a cigarette and lights it, then passes it to me saying it will calm me down. I take a long drag and immediately start coughing; it is not like the cigarettes I have smoked before. My boyfriend asks me if it is the first time I have smoked pot. I nod, he laughs, his friend tells me to have another drag and settle back for the ride.

The room is spinning like crazy now and even when I close my eyes it does not stop. It is like my recurring nightmare, only worse, because this is real life and I have no idea how to stop it. Someone has put a bucket next to me just in case I throw up so I must look quite sick. I notice my knickers are on

Fourteen

the floor but I am not sure how they got there. My boyfriend is on top of me and spreads my legs apart and pushes his dick inside me. All I can do is try not to vomit and hope he is wearing a condom. He finishes and pretty quickly falls asleep. I cuddle for a little bit but then a wave of nausea hits me and I pull myself over to the bucket. I am not sick but I rest my head near it and almost fall asleep with a little smile on my face, thinking I must look like that other guy hugging the ice-cream container.

Suddenly, I am pulled off the couch and my face is pushed down on the floor. I struggle to turn around and see what is happening but someone pushes my face back to the floor and ties cloth around my mouth. They grab my arms. They push my legs apart. I try to struggle, to scream, to stop whatever is happening, to turn around, but the room is still spinning and my stomach is churning and they are much too strong for me. They thrust and grunt. It seems like forever. My head hits the iron leg of the couch, my twisted arms are burning in their sockets and my body is hurting and shivering and stinging and raw. For a moment I seem to lose consciousness and think I see Astintina hovering beside me.

I know it is over when the back door slams shut. I have vomited on the cloth in my mouth. I take it off, drop it into the bucket and am sick again. I

Heartless

put on my knickers, my jeans, my top, my jumper, my boyfriend's jumper, my boyfriend's jacket. I pull these clothes close around me. Everyone is sleeping. My boyfriend is sleeping. Peacefully. His growing red heart is drowsy, lethargic, beating sluggish but constant. I lay my head on his chest to feel the soothing, thumping resonance, hoping it will show mine how not to care, how not to fill with loathing, how not to hold sorrow, but it offers no solace.

Mum is still asleep when I get home so I cannot have a shower. I fill the hand basin and try as much as I can to scrub myself with the flannel. I do it for three hours until the sun comes up but I still feel filthy, soiled, diseased.

When I vomit up my breakfast in the morning, Mum lets me have the day off. I have three showers during the day. I wash my clothes twice in the washing machine. I find Mum's cigarettes and smoke six of them. Then I throw up again and again, desperately trying to get it all out, to purify, to expel, to purge out the hideous rot inside me.

My heart barely beats the whole time, bits of her turning into cold stone. Silent and subdued and resenting and ashamed. Always ashamed. I write in my diary about my heart's shame. About how my heart will punish me now. How she will ache not just in the night-time now, but every minute

Fourteen

of every hour of every day just to spite me. How her shame pulses round my body and lodges in my shoulders and makes me walk around stooped with the weight of it. And how I wish, how I wish, how I wish, that she was not mine. That I did not have a heart at all. That I was heartless.

twenty-one

No one thought I would make it through the rest of high school, let alone get accepted into university. I certainly had my doubts, seeing as though I spent more time drinking and sedating and smoking and forgetting and doing whatever else was going, than putting my head into books. I was under the distinct impression that no longer was a distinguished and celebrated Great Life Purpose reserved for me. It seemed quite clear that the fiendish hands of Fate had weaved a vastly different outcome for my life and no matter how much my wretched heart protested and pounded, then ached and cowered, events would constantly unfold to resoundingly prove my road would ultimately come to a dead end. And I had, by and large, resigned myself to this fact.

Out of the blue, one act of kindness saved me.

Bestowed upon at the beginning of upper high school, by a big, bespectacled substitute English teacher named Mr Simmons. Given one term to whip us into a halfway decent creative writing shape, he commanded us to write a short story of Hope over the course of a month for homework. Needless to say, inspiration was readily unavailable to me and the silly concept did little to invoke it. Three days before the assignment was due, I finally put pen to paper.

I told the tale of a partially blind, orphaned girl who had lost her right arm in the grisly car accident that also claimed the lives of her parents. Facing trial after tribulation, the girl is driven to contemplate suicide. The night before her designated day of self-destruction, a world-weary and haggard man appears at her door. He reveals he is her father, mistakenly presumed dead through a hospital records debacle. After a long period of amnesia caused by the collision, he finally had a blinding epiphany and remembered her existence. He cried out, his face skyward.

Praise the Lord!

For the next ten years, fuelled by a fierce love and desperate loyalty, the devoted father had searched the world to find her and at last was here, reunited with his long, lost, lonesome daughter. They held

Twenty-one

each other and wept, then danced and laughed, and the story ended in a shower of soft tissues and surging violins.

Epic, emotional and bursting at the binding with important adjectives from the biggest thesaurus I could find, I thought it was a pile of torrid crap confirming I could never be a writer of any true merit. But Mr Simmons adored it. So much so that he secretly entered it into a prestigious creative writing competition for upper high-school students. At the end of the term, just days before he was due to leave, the notice came through that I had won a Highly Commended Award, in the form of a very official-looking certificate, stuck to the inside cover of an intriguing collection of marvellous Edgar Allan Poe short stories. When Mr Simmons gave it to me, he looked me squarely in the eye, shook my hand and congratulated me, almost as if I were a peer. Then, he whisked me up into a wonderfully warm hug.

I am very proud of you, very proud. You should be very proud of yourself. See what you can do? See? Don't sell yourself short, dear girl, don't sell yourself short.

While his words were soft and kind and soothing to hear, it was the hug that had profound consequences. Wrapped up and tucked away in big, solid, shielding arms, every fibre in my body softened and every cell in my structure settled. For that sweet moment, my aching heart was sedated and I surrendered to a quiet swelling of peace. In these comforting arms of acknowledgment, I felt the surge of a begrudging pledge to myself that if this was the reward, then maybe I should try my best after all. And as steadfastly as I could, I carried this with me through my remaining high-school roller-coaster years, and it pulled me across the percentage line in important exams and it scraped me through the threshold to an Arts degree at a big-city university. Maybe I would begin my Great Life Purpose after all.

And here I am. Sitting, slightly stoned, on the very edge of a resplendent set of jagged, dramatic city cliffs. The ocean thunders and booms, rumbles and growls underneath me, thrusting showers of salty spray through my drug-hazed aura, cleansing me, reviving me, reminding me. I look down and feel the magnetic pull of this almighty force, and I draw from it again that familiar masochistic comfort of knowing it will always be there, ready and raging and willing to provide, when required, a gloriously theatrical end. Someday soon, I write in my white regulation uni student diary.

Until then, the twinkling of too many living-

Twenty-one

room lights illuminates the neighbouring urban hills. So many people, living, breathing, coughing, chortling, giggling, spluttering, stumbling through life, all the while losing dead skin and hair. So many stories, tragedies, farces. Rollicking romance novels and sterile technical manuals. Proud, multi-generational family sagas and three-line, obligatory newspaper obituaries. So many variations of citified hearts with their incessant beating, some loud and some meek, some angry and some greedy, some needy and some lovely. Some facilely stupefied like mine.

Yet here I am.

*

Dad will not be able to make it to my graduation. Another frightfully important, amazing milestone, once-in-a-lifetime occurrence, simply too-breathtakingly-significant-to-miss event has arisen on the same date. My stepbrother's Under-Fourteen Boys Australian Rules Football Semi-Final. As the vital key reserve, dutiful sitter for three-quarters of the game on the sidelines, staggeringly valuable bench player that my stepbrother is, my dad was naturally torn between a rock and a hard place. Really. But, as we all know, with competition being so fierce and cut-throat at this level of the game, it may very well be the last time that the Under-Fourteen Boys Mayfair Little Devils get to play for the rest of the year. And who knows if they will be able to assemble such a formidable team next year. So Dad is compelled to stay and watch and support and sanctify his only son in this worthy endeavour, and miss that daughter from the other marriage's University Graduation Day.

Mum is coming, though. Wild horses would not keep her away. She who thought, at so many treacherous forks in my turbulent road, that I would be lost, left, luckless in life, shines now when she thinks of me. She who thought, each time she found my bed empty at midnight, that I would be pregnant, penniless and a pariah at seventeen, swells with pride when she talks of her university-educated daughter. She who thought, as both of our battered hearts shrivelled and fell silent and shut up shop, that we would be worn, wasted and left behind, floods with relief when she realises there may be a future of sorts after all.

Mum sits upright, three rows from the back, amongst a respectable collection of similarly pleased parents, who may or may not understand just what it means for my mother to be there. Pulsing with a palpable pride, her shining eyes spotlight me as I walk on air to the podium and I feel every ounce of

Twenty-one

my flesh and soul wired with her admiration. I do all I can to resist the urge to drop to my knees and sprawl prostrate in gushing gratitude to the graceful power that made it turn out this way. Shaking, I accept my degree, have my photo taken and see in the stars flashing before my eyes, Astintina. Her heart beams light once more to mine and for a divine moment, a blessed suspension of disbelief, I feel as if I am the child with the big, loud, red, dancing heart again.

As the crowd slowly thins, my mum holds me tight for the longest time. I feel her fragile frame, wrapped in a new cream blouse and pleated skirt bought for more than she could afford, her heart hammering with unfamiliar happiness.

I'm just so . . . it's all just so, you know.

I know, Mum.

I just never thought, you know . . . that you'd be—

I know, Mum, me too.

It's just that when you were younger you were such a bright little girl and then, you know, we were by ourselves and you would get so . . . I wouldn't know what to do.

Well, you did a good job, Mum.

D'you think so?

I'm here, aren't I?

But then, inevitably, throughout the following day, the magic slowly dissipates, the disbelief seeps back in and reality pulls all into sharp focus as I contemplate the career options afforded me with an Arts degree. I watch as the heady euphoria surrounding Mum from the previous day's pride and joy slowly diffuses, sending her in a slow-motion spin back down to earth. I see those nervous little flutterings sift fleetingly again through her heart and I hear it murmur conspiringly to mine to not be fooled, that the road is still long and arduous, and that the day is still really night in disguise. Then, just past midnight, as the witches come out to play and I, in my sleep, wield my ever-ready and present steak knife at their shadows, Mum's heart has an attack.

*

The hospital smells are as bad as I remember, perhaps even more so, with the enormous number of people flooding through the space. A big-city hospital reeks not only of relentless hordes of sick people and medicine and cleaning products but, underneath it all, a sinister odour of something else. Like metaphysical staphylococci, clusters of fear crowd the corridors. Not simply the fear of pain and dying, but the more elusive, lower-resonating,

Twenty-one

trembling fear of dying here, in this big-city obscurity, in this sea of mass indifference. Yet one more of many who will shuffle off today in listless anonymity. Dying here, amongst too many, plagued by that nagging, gnawing, gaping fear that the whole thing was really quite pointless after all.

Luckily, it was not Mum's time to face those fears. Whatever it was that attacked Mum's heart was only mildly aggressive, not intent on killing. Perhaps a cunning ploy to weaken the defences for a more resounding blow at a later stage. Perhaps merely a scare tactic, a reminder of ever-present mortality, delivered with a benevolent motive in mind, to remind of the preciousness of life and to kick-start that unfulfilled spirit and its desolated heart into action.

As I inhaled long and ponderously on my cigarette, sitting in the hospital back alley among laundry trolleys and trash units, writing a stream of aimless consciousness in my diary, I mused. Perhaps it was the heart attacking itself. Back in the glory days of imaginary friend communication, Astintina surmised that Mum's heart had forgotten how to jump for joy and the spasms she had then were desperate attempts by the heart to try and remember. I saw clearly, prophetically, at that age, that Mum's heart was scared of something but I did not know what until I saw Dad kissing the eventual stepmother on our couch. So perhaps, finally, Mum's heart has had enough, and has chosen the only way out it can see, attacking itself in a strange yet valiant attempt at suicide. Or, as these things often are, perhaps this is a lonely heart's forlorn cry for help, 'please, please, someone', before despair drowns out her last breath of life.

Placing the call to Dad was strangely difficult. Over the last fourteen years, we have very rarely spoken about Mum. I certainly have never actively sought to make the two connect; in fact, quite the opposite, have conscientiously avoided discussing in any detail the life I lived with Mum. Not that unusual, considering it was not exactly the bold and bright and beaming life of happy and exciting discussion. Considering, too, that I have never really had time alone with my dad since I was seven and that I always felt revealing my other life with Mum in front of the new family would have been like slowly undressing to complete nakedness, pointing out every flaw, blemish, rash, boil, scar, sore on my body and inviting the onlookers to scratch at, then throw salt on, every last little wound they could find.

Hey Dad, d'you have a second to talk?
Hang on, I'll just . . . the cricket's on, last six overs.

Twenty-one

Mum had a heart attack last night.
Who . . . your mother?
Yes, Mum.
Oh . . .
She's all right though, it was apparently a mild one.
That's good then.
Just thought you might like to know.
Yeah, thanks love. Geez . . .
Yeah . . . So . . . How'd the boys' semi-final go?
Gave the other team a hiding.
So they made it through to the grand final?
Easily.
That's good then.
It was. The boys were rapt.
I bet they were.
Oh, that's right, how'd the graduation go?
Good Dad, thanks.
Good.
Yeah, good to be finally finished.
I bet. What's next?
Oh, you know, try and get my writing out there.
What about for money?
Oh, actually, I'm starting a temporary waitressing job next week. Just temporary.
Good.
Yeah. Well, I'd better go.

Yeah, well, tell your mother I hope she feels better.
Will do.

I stubbed out my cigarette. I had been trying not to think about the inauspicious start to my adult working life, not as a writer with a Great Life Purpose, but as a waitress struggling to make ends meet in the real world. I pulled out another cigarette.

Emphysema is a truly terrible thing to experience, I would imagine.

I rolled my eyes and huffed a muttering sigh.
Oh please.

I turned to confront the would-be lecturer. And there he was. An Adonis attached to an angel's voice. Leaning casually out of the doorway. Holding a dripping green garbage bag. Raising one rugged eyebrow. Teasing me with the hint of the cheekiest grin. Yes, there he was. The most Beautiful Man I had ever seen. It was undeniable. It was clear as day. It was so very plain to see. For there, as irrefutable proof, on the white starchy cuff of his left sleeve, was the picture-perfect projection of his luminous, effulgent and awesomely deep red heart. I tell him.

You'll be pleased to know I'm giving up the smokes tomorrow.

My Beautiful Man was not much older than me and was halfway through an arduous medical degree, with a fervent desire to specialise in heart

Twenty-one

surgery. Only once thus far had he been privy to what he described as a Divine Moment. During a first-hand observation of a heart transplant, he had been allowed to hold the patient's still-beating heart aloft from its natural home in the chest cavity. With shining eyes and an excited heart, he told of holding this most precious entity, feeling its mystical power and profound force as it courageously continued to pound out its life-affirming beat in his hands. He told of a celestial energy that radiated from this heart, revealing to him in a beam of brilliant truth that buried deep within these muscle folds, protected, sheltered, cloistered, was the eternal soul itself. And even more, that one could understand the spirit and secrets of a soul by the health and hues of its heart.

I nodded in adoring agreement and silently vowed to never show him mine.

*

Walking up the crisp and cared-for garden path of his family home, I forced myself to fixate on a row of budding gardenias, commenting effusively on their delicate beauty whilst bending down to gulp up their fragrance, all in a desperate attempt to stall time and get oxygen to my brain. The closer we were getting to the door, the faster the panic over meeting his parents was rising. My scaredy-cat clawing heart was again doing her old trick of leaping into my mouth and drumming dread through my body, making me want to throw up on their sweet, old-style front porch.

Performing respectfully well in nice and polite social situations has never been my particular forte and today it mattered more than anything that I put on a decent show. I loved this Beautiful Man. Every ounce of me, every fibre, nerve, cell, synapse and soft tissue loved him. Every element of me, every jaded thought, cynical smirk and sceptical feeling loved him. Even my mute and mutilated little heart loved him. I could tell, for her aches ebbed slightly when he was around and she would peer out sneakily from her fifth-rib hiding place to steal a quick glance at his sleeve, just to see for a moment that ever-present projection of his handsome heart worn proudly on it.

We paused before knocking on the door and he held my hand so tight our pulses mingled. He pressed the cheery doorbell. Noisy eruptions of joie de vivre shot through the front door. A dog barking, paws running, stairs creaking, voices yelling.

I'm getting the muffins out!
Where's Dad?
Jazzy's pooed on the floor!

Twenty-one

They're at the door!
The tray's hot!
They'll step on it if I don't get it now!
I've got a towel on my head!
Ow shit, I burnt myself!
Wasn't it at one?
It is one!
My bloody watch has stopped!

The door is flung open by a pocket rocket of a first-rate woman with her hair wrapped in a bright yellow daffodil towel, accompanied by a massively pawed licking machine of a boisterous black labrador.

Don't panic!

She kisses me then kisses her son and the dog does the same.

Your sister just rescued her muffins, Dad just spotted Jazzy's poo on the floor and I just got out of the shower in the nick of time, so it's a big bloody success already, thank god! Come in!

What an afternoon we had. No trace of any nice and polite social gathering in this home. Instead, an all-in-together romp of spilled drinks, slobbering dog, strident laughter and snug family. We smoked up piles of onion on the barbecue, popped a champagne cork into the neighbour's backyard, slipped Jazzy sausages under the table until she was sick and ate every last freshly baked sister's special muffin. I was taken on a tour through the trucks and bones and special rocks in his old bedroom, shown every photo of him as the cute-as-pie baby to sticking-out-ears child to pimply embarrassed adolescent ever taken and heard all his ratbag stories of broken limbs and vomiting and last-minute homework and pretend surgery on his younger sister.

Throughout the afternoon, every little thing, and all around it, was easiness and comfortableness. Warm and ripe in the air was the assurance of a complete family. The bits-and-pieces-laden walls spoke of safety, touching memories and togetherness. The well-trodden pathways in the carpet showed the family tradition of happy play and flowing life. Spirits flourished and souls sang and hearts danced here. So much so that everyone in this family wore the projection of their heart on their sleeve, like my Beautiful Man. Everyone had a deep red and healthy heart that they listened to and loved, that held no shame or fear or scarring, that they were rightfully proud to show to the planet. Compassionate hearts that shined a light on the world and set an example for all to aspire to. Including me. How I yearned for what they had.

While I laughed and played that afternoon, and basked in their kindness, and felt a freedom long

Twenty-one

forgotten, and admired the majesty of their hearts, I did not dare to reveal my own. And even though I felt her sway and quiver and chance to dream, I did not dare wear her on my sleeve. I did not want to be turned away just yet. I did not want to be found out just yet. I did not want the unhealthy hues of my heart to give away the troubled secrets of my soul just yet.

As she showed me to the door, my Beautiful Man's mother rubbed my back.

You carry a lot of tension there, darling.
Oh, really?
The world on your shoulders.
Oh, well, you know, rent, bills, life.
You don't live at home?
No, Mum lives a couple of hours north of the city.
With Dad?
Um, no.

I looked to my Beautiful Man to move the conversation along; he was nose-deep in happy dog. His mother's shining blue eyes pierced into mine and I held my breath, hoping my heart was well hidden.

Um, no, he lives interstate.
When did that happen?
Um, oh, when I was about seven.
Ah, 'Show me the boy . . .'
Sorry?

Not to worry, precious girl, it's all going to be all right.

She smiled and my heart jolted with the electric shock of this unexpected show of love, sending me flushed and tripping down the front porch steps, into the arms of my Beautiful Man and Jazzy's relentless wet kisses.

*

Three photographs travel with me everywhere. They are the only depictions I have of my family, in the early days, when we were a family. And they are the only portals to that time I have left. I cannot seem to remember any other fragments of scenes or moments anymore, apart from the day Dad left.

On the back of the first photograph, Mum has written 'six months'. I am swathed up cosy and snug, lying on Mum's lap as she sorts through a messy pile of official-looking papers on the floor. Dad squats beside her, rattling a furry toy in front of me while pulling a tongue-poking peekaboo face. The second one is a stiflingly formal family portrait and plainly written across both my mum and dad's faces is the furrowed frown of 'can we really afford this?'

The photograph I look at the most is the third one. I am about five, dressed in my all-time favourite, baby-pink ballerina tutu, pulled down over the

Twenty-one

top of my all-time favourite bright orange with blue flowers full-piece bathing suit. I am standing, pleased as punch and proud of myself, in front of the mirror at Mum's dresser with half my face painted in her siren-red lipstick and her black-feathered, good going-out comb stuck lopsidedly in my hair. Dad stands next to me, his hands on his hips and his head thrown back in the throes of an all-encompassing, from the bottom of the belly, laugh. Mum can be seen in the reflection of the mirror with an enormous grin, holding a clean-me-up flannel towel and haphazardly taking the photo.

I like to fall asleep with this image in my mind. While it can never really appease the monotonous persistence of my heart's ache, it occasionally manages to form a peculiarly peaceful bubble of calm around my imagination, so that the dark and all its tricks cannot take over my mind and taunt me into fits and starts. But no matter how comforting its story, the photo could never hold enough power to loosen my night-time grip on that trusty steak knife. Only my Beautiful Man can do that.

He has slept over twice and even though we have not made love yet, he spends the whole night in my bed, lying close to me, touching me, holding me, softly imbibing me with the sweetest manna from the most splendid heavens. The first night,

I did not sleep at all. I did not dare miss a minute of such bliss. I gazed at his beautiful heart, mesmerised, awestruck. It was big and strong, steady and true, realised and ripened. I touched it ever so lightly and an electric current of affection seared through me and I lost my breath and averted my eyes. It whispered it would give itself to me and then smiled at me with a love so profound, of almost unfathomable depth, it was all I could do to prevent my heart from leaping into his hands for the rest of her life.

To stop this from happening again, the second time he slept over, I banned myself from looking at his heart and made myself fall asleep. That night, I dreamt of Astintina. I was lying on a stone-cold concrete slab in a damp and dark chamber, quite sure I was about to die. Then, a light switched on overhead, only it was not an actual light, it was the beacon-bright body of Astintina. As she hovered over me, a form began to take shape around her. I started to breathe heavy and frantically tear at my chest as I recognised who she had conjured. It was my Beautiful Man. Astintina sat at his right breast and watched as golden lightning bolts fired from his heart directly at mine, trying to revive her. My heart had fallen from a great height during the night before and was lying unconscious in my chest

Twenty-one

cavity. The rib cage had closed around her like an iron lung capsule to protect her from predators while she recovered. And even though I knew this covering was keeping my heart safe, I also knew I had to try and quickly prise it open before Astintina faded away, taking my Beautiful Man with her. I scratched until my skin was red raw.

And woke up, still scratching. Breathing fast and heavy. Reaching for him. Mercifully, he was there. Laying tranquil in untarnished slumber, a slowly rising and falling body of sweet lines and soft curves. My Beautiful Man. I decided to stay up and write all about him and his electrifying heart in my diary.

*

This Christmas, I have decided not to visit my Dad. Every year past, I have made the hopeful pilgrimage in some vain attempt to experience a special connection of meaning with him. And every year past, I have been starkly reminded that my devout journey is meaningless, that my prayers are aimed at a false god who never actually existed and that I really am much better off dropping my illusions and accepting an atheistic view of reality. My decision rolls in like the sudden rush of a rogue wave, dumping me in a whitewash of churning sadness and resigned relief.

Heartless

My mum has decided not to put up a Christmas tree this year. In fact, there are no decorations whatsoever, except for the battered old plastic Santa face, with textaed-in eyelashes, that has always commanded a leering position over the infrequent visitors at the front door. A wise decision, considering there is no space left in her trinket-ridden house. Over the past few years, every lonely weekend, Mum has taken to hanging out in second-hand shops and buying their stuff. Ceramic dogs, glass angels, hanging tea towels, teddy bears and dolls of all shapes and sizes, miniature vases, commemorative spoons, porcelain cups and saucers, plastic farmyard animals and flying wooden ducks. Every last little bit of the place is now covered with several hours a day's worth of dusting work.

Christmas morning is a quiet affair. We decide not to have anything fancy, just a bowl of cereal and a piece of toast with strawberry jam. I consume three cups of instant coffee and still achieve nowhere near the caffeine hit I need to function with a modicum of sense. The radio plays the familiarly cheesy, dusted-off-once-a-year, frightfully annoying festive tunes, commentated on through the clenched teeth of an unlucky disc jockey who is either out of favour with the boss or in dire need of a doubled-up dollar.

Twenty-one

Mum and I exchange our gifts of perfume and underwear and books and mandatory chocolate. I cannot help but fuel the trinket addiction with a small family of pink flying pottery pigs. She takes a quick photo of me, then I take a quick photo of her, sitting in our wrapping paper rubbish. She packs me a lunch for the four-hour bus trip south to the big city. She wishes me luck for the Christmas dinner with my Beautiful Man's family and I cross my fingers with a grimacing smile. Before I go, she hands me a rolled up poster in brown paper and red ribbon and tells me not to open it until I go to bed tonight and that I need to put it up somewhere special to look at if I am ever feeling low. She is so sentimental I wonder if she needs her medication readjusted. Then, I leave her alone to switch on the television, settle in for the midday movie and count out her heart pills into the appropriate sections of her per-week pill container.

Walking up the driveway of my Beautiful Man's family home I feel a lightning quick sting in the back of my eyes and a fizzy tingling through my nose and I have to take three deep breaths to stop myself from crying. The house looks so wonderfully happy. Big-nosed plastic reindeers flash red lights in the front windows. Glittering gold and green tinsel shines a sparkling border around the window frames. A massive movie-size Christmas tree stands centre stage covered in fake cotton wool snow and cheerfully cheeky swaying Santas. Several long lines of hanging Christmas cards announce a treasured family well loved by so very many. And I wonder, no matter how badly I want to, if I could ever really fit in here.

Choosing Christmas presents for this family had been an agonising day-long diabolical procedure and in the end, I opted for the tried and tested line-up of usual suspects. His mum got an inoffensively light popular perfume, his dad a casual blue short-sleeved summer shirt and his sister an easy and ordinary, anyone-could-wear, mascara and lip gloss combination. For my Beautiful Man, I got a mischievous pair of Superman briefs with matching socks and an incomprehensible to the layman heart transplant methodology report I stumbled across at the university bookshop. And, of course, something special, something private, something possibly embarrassing, for later. Everyone loved everything, they said.

Then they gave me their gifts. First, from the sister, a beautifully bound in soft leather, faded burgundy writing book which could be clasped closed by a delicate bronze butterfly.

For all those cool books you're going to write in the future.

Twenty-one

I guffawed.

Yeah, when I have time off from my real job as a waitress!

From his mother, an exquisite silver pendant bearing a potent turquoise gemstone.

Turquoise is a powerful healing stone that will help you fully embrace and express yourself.

I felt a hive of nerves slowly work up my neck.

Oh, well, that could be dangerous!

And from his father, a raggedly little rascal of a teddy bear with scruffed-up ears and sink-into-me eyes.

For those nights when you need the company.

Poor thing! He's going to have his work cut out for him!

My head was beginning to spin. Then, from my Beautiful Man, an enchanting fairytale of a golden charm bracelet, adorned with alchemical trinkets of suns and moons and stars and magic.

And I lost my orientation altogether. I felt as if I were in an alien world where people were always wonderful and kind and generous. A world where people gave each other the most amazing gifts as a matter of course, because they could and wanted to and loved to watch the recipient light up with glee. A world where hugs and laughter and intimate connections were commonplace. A world where the fecund atmosphere of positivity was so thick, it was a virtual humidicrib of happiness. So thick I almost could not breathe.

In the dry climate that I knew, where harsh winds of negativity blew with mundane regularity, the air was arid, unkind, unforgiving. In that desert landscape only jagged scrawny things could grow, patchy, uneven, sparse. My world was a toughened terrain bereft of lush embraces and blossoming joy. Sitting here, in my Beautiful Man's world, I felt like an impostor. I did not know how to relax and simply be in this world. How to let its glorious sunlight nurture me, bud me and bring me to bloom.

So, with these heartfelt gifts laid before me deserving my grateful attention, all I could do was quickly guzzle down my soft drink in a nervous fluster. Then, as I went to say thanks, the carbonated gas rushed back up my throat and before a word was said I began choking and spluttering and squashing down burps as best I could.

I'm sorry.

I rushed to the bathroom and coughed up roast carrot and pea mush and strips of my trachea. My eyes were running and my nose was weeping and my face was beetroot red. I looked at myself in the mirror. There she was. An ugly, unsightly yucca of a

Twenty-one

girl. No graceful gardenia of temperate climate here. Just me, only me, pathetic, undeserving, there really was no escaping it. I sucked up as much armoured nonchalance as I could and strolled back in.

Wow, that gas, hey. Nearly knocked me out. But thanks for the pressies. They're really cool.

My Beautiful Man came back to my flat that night and I snuggled up in bed as close to him as I could, trying to bury myself in his grace.

I'm sorry for making such a fool out of myself.

No you didn't, you were funny.

No, I was an embarrassment.

Did you like the presents?

They're so great.

Mum was worried you didn't like them.

I love them, I love them so much. I've never been given presents like that before.

I've got something else I want to give you but I didn't want to do it at dinner.

Me too, I've got you something else too.

Well, you first.

No, you go.

No, ladies first.

I rolled my eyes and sighed and pulled out from my bedside drawer a little box wrapped in red shiny paper with a tiny gold bow on it.

It's okay if you don't like it.

He daintily removed the tiny gold bow, then carefully pulled back the sticky tape without tearing the paper. When he saw the box he shot me a terrific smile. I folded my arms tight into my chest, pretending I was cold, but mainly to keep my pounding heart from popping out. He opened the box and let out a little gasp. He gently pulled out the gift and placed it lovingly on the pad of his fingertip. It fit there perfectly, small but flawless, a pure rose-gold love heart.

It's beautiful.

He gazed at it a long, long time.

Then he turned his attention back to me.

I have something similar to give to you. Only it's not exactly gold. And I don't know if . . . you may not actually want it, I don't know. But I want you to keep it for a few days, at least, just until I get back from holidays in four days . . . you can give it back then if you decide it's not for you . . . but right now, I just . . . I really want you to have it. I know it was meant for you.

He took a deep breath. His hands were trembling. He fixed me with a gaze that lasered clean through my shut-tight rib cage, pushed aside my protective left lung and penetrated straight into the very petrified heart of me. He took another deep breath. Then he reached into himself, cradled his

Twenty-one

own heart in both hands, brought it out into the open and laid it bare at my feet.

I give you my heart.

*

For that first day, I floated on a tremendous heaven-sent cloud, emanating from the aura of my Beautiful Man's angelic heart. It filled me with an indescribable cocktail of sensations from joy to contentment to certainty to wonderment to fulfilment. I soared high on a wing of undying devotion to this godly heart, far higher than any drug had ever taken me. I scaled euphoric heights and gazed at the vista stretching before me, a majestic grand canyon of a magical life created exclusively for me by my Beautiful Man's supreme heart.

What a heart! The rare, singular beauty of it. The natural strength of solid character held within it. The way it pounded out with such vigour and delight an enthralling beat all its own. The way its compelling enthusiasm enticed all to it and opened them to a gilded realm where dreams came true. The sheer vitality of its colours and hues, a vibrant testament to its robust health. And, of course, with such a brilliant palette painting this heart to perfection, what must the precious soul encased within be like. On and on I floated that day.

On the second day, I gradually drifted back to a less ethereal plane, like a goose feather falling in a slow-motion spiral down to its soft doona. It was not that my Beautiful Man's heart had lost any of its regal grandeur, nor lessened in its intense magnetism. On the contrary, its allure had continued to pulse out on ever-expanding circles of influence. Its call to life was still loud and clear and committed. But, as the light of day began to fade, something cold, something insidious, something insistent, began to curl around me. It whispered to my carefree cells a foreboding message of caution. It told my elated atoms to be wary, to keep my guard up, because someone like me could not stay in such light for long. It told me I would not be able to keep up with its brilliance; I would burn, blister and become even uglier in the face of this flame. All through the night this creeping serpent of trepidation coiled around me, applying its subtle squeeze, softly choking the last wisps of hope and possibility from my lungs.

On the third day, I stowed my Beautiful Man's heart away in a cupboard. I thought about my own heart. Now a shadow of her former self, I remembered her shrouds of fear and blankets of shame. All her broken-off pieces never found, leaving perpetually rotting wounds in their place. Her battered chambers and bruised ventricles, her decrepit veins

Twenty-one

and torn-up aorta. Her limping, hiding, crippled way of pumping out her stunted beat.

Then I thought about what this heart said of my soul. I remembered all the times I had sought to obliterate myself, drunken and drugged and desperate to drown out my sorry self. All my tragic liaisons with types who kept closed hearts or mean hearts or stupid hearts, and my smug security in knowing they would never have any interest in mine. I remembered that night at a boyfriend's house when I was used like a disposable nothing and the resounding confirmation it shouted in my being of my true worthlessness, my shamefulness, my lowliness.

And I thought about when Dad left. How I tried to be the most beautiful, adorable, lovable thing he ever saw and how I truly believed it would be enough to make him stay. How I failed dismally, proving that I was not anywhere near worthy enough, not anywhere near pretty enough or shiny enough. How I was not even a little bit, the tiniest speck, of something wonderful enough that my father would stay and would want to love.

This was the truth of my self, of my soul and of my heart. How could I ever show this to my Beautiful Man and his breathtaking heart? How could I ever fit into his noble family of fine hearts? If I ever revealed the ugly truth of me and my mangled heart, they would gasp in shock and recoil in horror. They would say they had been deceived, that I was an undeserving, despicable fraud. My Beautiful Man would be ill with repulsion and loathing and disgust. He would marvel at how very close he came to giving his pristine heart to an irredeemable defective. He would turn and leave. Like my dad.

And I would not blame him. And I will spare him the trouble.

*

On the fourth day, my Beautiful Man came to see me. I told him that while his heart was very special, it was not the heart for me. I told him that he should find someone who was a proper match for his heart, because ours would just never get along. I told him that he was wrong in his judgment when he thought that his heart was meant for me. I told him that he should take his heart back and leave.

As he took his heart out of my hands, it broke completely in two. Ashen-faced and hunched over, he placed his broken heart back into his body. He gave me a look laden with pain and confusion and sadness and humiliation and it wrenched my heart into my throat and cracked her into pieces. Without a word, he left.

Twenty-one

For the next six months I felt my heart keep bleeding and bleeding. She finally bled dry and seemed to shrivel to the size and texture of a dried-up pea. I wrote long passages of my Beautiful Man in my leather-bound burgundy diary, of how much I loved him and how I had broken his heaven-sent heart. I wrote of my cruelty, my callousness, my unforgivable unkindness to the most Beautiful Man I had ever seen, the only man I had ever loved. I wrote that maybe now I had finally achieved what I had long since wanted. To be completely and utterly heartless.

twenty-eight

THE FIRST THING I notice is how disgustingly sticky these sheets are and I realise I must be in someone else's bed. A psychedelically strobing bedside clock flashes 4:07 next to me and I assume it implies ante meridiem because the room is pitch-black and the strange body in bed with me is snoring. The sweetly-sick stench of alcohol saturates the air and it takes every ounce of focused mind control to stifle my rising queasiness, encourage some semblance of unsteady equilibrium and haul myself out of this other person's scarily festering futon bed.

I have no idea where I am and while I wait for my eyes to attempt to see in the dark, I flick through the cluttered-up filing cabinet in my shambolic brain to hopefully find an answer. Bar, vodka, builder type, brawny biceps with calloused hands, gunmetal

Holden ute, grungy urban flat, Jim Beam, bucket bong, farcically quick sex, dirty toilet, good idea unable to be remembered, joint, room spinning, distastefully wet kissing, file ends.

I can just make out my little black dress and faded denim jacket on the floor in front of me, and as I pick them up as painfully quietly as possible, I fumble blindly for my purple strapless kitten heels. Most importantly, with a great wash of relief, I finally find my purple lace knickers partially kicked under the flea-bitten futon. With as much slow stealth as I can muster, so as not to wake the hairier-than-I-remembered, sleeping freight train next to me, I place each one of my three twittering bronze bangles in their own separate pocket of my purple pretend-Gucci handbag and, in tiny increments, ease off the bed and onto the even stickier shag-pile carpet. Clutching my stuff in one hand and letting the other feel its way on the floor, I do my absolute best not to imagine what lives in this rank forest of a floor covering. I crawl into the passageway and onto the cold tiles of the kitchen where thankfully the front door is.

Seedy yellow light from the outside stairwell casts a jaundiced pallor over the already hideously ill-looking kitchen. The only mild consolation I can find is that it closely matches the way I currently

Twenty-eight

feel about myself. Rancid. It seems I can always trust my shot-with-holes instincts to nose their way into a rat's nest, like I clearly did last night. I hastily put my clothes on, carry my heels so as not to disturb him, avoid the mirror at all costs and take the last twenty bucks from his wallet on the table. Even though they are not my ideal brand, I take his cigarettes as well.

Immediately upon stepping out onto the street, I land my foot in a pile of broken beer bottle and a nasty piece wedges itself into the delicate skin between my big and second toes. Luckily, the alcohol in my blood is still thick enough to dull the pain and after I pull the glass out, only a relentless throbbing and rivulet of blood signals to my brain that this actually hurts. Letting it rest while the blood coagulates, I sit on the cleanest patch of street kerb I can find and smoke a cigarette. My memory is about to wander back to a certain hospital alleyway seven years ago, but I will not let it.

Four blocks away from my own grungy inner-city studio apartment, the taxi pulls over. It has driven me as far as twenty bucks will allow. As the cab drives off, I button up tight my denim jacket, lace my door keys through my knuckles just in case, grip my bag close with the other hand and limp as quickly as I can to my place. But not so quickly that

I look like I am scared. I breathe in deep the freezing air to clear my head and I concentrate hard on looking like I am someone you do not want to mess with. I stir myself up in my mind, thinking of all the fucked-up things in the world that fill me with rage, all the injustice, abuse, war, rape, abandonment, and I begin to grit my teeth with the feeling that right now, I could pick a fight and actually win.

Shadows jump out at me from apartment building pathways; I soldier on. Two street lamps are out and another flickers, making it hard to discern what that shape is crouching near the bus stop. I grip my keys hard in my fist, prepare myself for a frightening confrontation and fix the stooping shape with my fiercest stare. As I get closer, the light suddenly blares on and I jump almost two feet into the air. The dreaded shape is a defaced post box. My split-pea wimp of a heart is flapping about mindlessly in my gut, stirring up the resident fear that nests there and making me want to hurl her up and out on the street. I light another cigarette in defiance, suck up the smoke long and hard, until she finally retreats dazed, in a nicotine haze, back behind her lung and shuts up.

Just as I make it to my building with my key at the ready, a hotted-up hoon car throbbing with thumping music and a smoking muffler cruises past, along

Twenty-eight

with the tediously obvious barrage of wolf whistles and obnoxious calls. One bleary-eyed obscenity of a human being sticks his offensively vulgar head out of his window.

Come on baby, come for a ride in our taxi to hell.
Get fucked, you ugly arsehole.
I'll fuck you, you fucking slut.

And he fumbles with the door handle. Too late; I am in my building and up the stairs quick sticks. A bottle smashes somewhere below but I am inside and safe. I double-check that I have my trusty steak knife at the ready to stash in my pillowcase. I note in my no-frills, plain-Jane supermarket-bought diary that I have miraculously made it yet again, foot injury and all, through another Night of the Long Walks Home.

Just as I am about to fall gratefully into bed, I knock my steak knife to the floor and it stabs the very same already-severed spot on my foot. This time, it lets me know how much it hurts and starts to bleed in furious protest. Cursing my clumsy stupidity, I search in my bathroom cupboard for a bandaid and catch a glimpse of myself in the mirror. Dark circles around my eyes, furrowed lines across my forehead, grey roots growing in my hair. All of it grotesque without and within, and I am not yet thirty. I can only stand to see that glimpse of myself for a second. And still, it is enough for the loathing to rise up seething, shuddering right through me, and I tell myself I probably should have taken that taxi ride to hell after all.

*

One week later and this damned foot is still throbbing. Usually, I sneak out of work to the back alley for no other legitimate reason than to indulge in a blessed cigarette. Tonight, crippled and cranky, I feel suitably justified in escaping yet another one of these interminable high-class society functions that seem to keep cropping up on my roster. Over the past seven years I have flitted from one waitressing gig to another, from cafes to business clubs to suburban pubs to corporate balls, and they are all as bad as each other. For seven years I have tried to keep tucked away safe in a corner of my mind the reassurance that this is not what I really do. That I am only passing the time and paying the rent until that real career comes along, something creative, something about writing, something that has shades of my once glorious Great Life Purpose about it.

But tonight, with my foot throbbing and my spirit tumbling, it is hard to keep up the optimism and I escape out the back before accidentally slipping and spilling red wine all over the clientele's starched-up

Twenty-eight

penguin suits and puffed-up ball gowns. Although, I will confess, it is quite a tempting scenario and still a strong possibility if another one of these arrogant arseholes brushes my tit again while I pour his stinking liquor. After seven long years, I am not sure how much more I can endure.

So, I hide in the shadows of the serving-class quarters and deeply, desperately, inhale a full lung of cigarette smoke to calm myself down. I take my working waitress flats off to give my foot a rest and feel relief flood over me. With my next puff, I think of my bottom drawer full of nowhere-near-finished manuscripts and resolve to start on them tomorrow. Yet another puff and I notice that familiar self-righteous Bolshevik sneer pull up and take aim at all those dogberry rich and their puerile pretensions inside. They would not know what a creative life means and what sacrifice it takes. They only know the charmed clinking of their silver platters and spoons. I wonder why it is I, of all people, who keeps getting landed with these bullshit functions. Must be that new bitch-face cow of a supervisor throwing her hefty-in-all-the-wrong-areas weight around. People! The world would be a kinder place without them. I breathe deep another drag.

It is an eerily beautiful night, still, a little steamy. A white-hot full moon glares down upon the skulking, nocturnal clutter of low life in these fermenting back alleys. The spooky sound of footsteps clangs on the cobblestone.

Mind if I bum one off you?

There he is, the Rugged Man. Looking begrudgingly dashing as any man in any uniform seems to, dressed in a jet-black valet's tux, hair slicked back, bowtie straight and neat. Looking the picture-perfect presentation of a model major lackey, but for one thing. Displayed proudly, pointedly, with the hint of rebellion, or the threat of mutiny lurking, his artist streak statement of non-conformity. A three-day growth dappled defiantly across his face. He pulls from his pocket a silver-plated, delicately etched, flip-lid cigarette lighter and suavely flicks it open like some devilish movie star from the smouldering forties.

Please, the performing monkey needs his nicotine hit.

Much later that night, after a diabolically long shift, a procession of ruddy-nosed and red pinot-lipped chauvinists and no less than seven sneaky cigarette rendezvous' with the Rugged Man, I sit on his armchair watching him fall asleep on his couch. He has regaled me for two thrilling hours with stories of mountains of money made and lost, whirlwind romances with famous ladies, being

Twenty-eight

within a fingertip of touching worldwide success, the addictive rush of transcendence in acting, the passionate pleasure of colour and texture on canvas, his as yet untapped avatar vision and where it may take him and the shiny path he hopes to walk to the very front door of his grand plans, if circumstances will allow. Which, so far, they have not. I nod with world-weary understanding.

As we smoke a little pot and pause for the playing of his favourite Miles Davis pieces, the Rugged Man tells me about himself. He is an actor and a painter, can improvise on the piano and the guitar, can speak a little French and a little bit less Spanish, is a yellow belt in some nearly forgotten form of karate, turned thirty-seven in March, has three planets in Pisces and a Scorpio Moon, cultivates a keen eye for expensive silver which he will collect when he can next afford to, was married once and will never do it again, left school when he was fourteen, got kicked out of home when he was fifteen, has barely spoken to his mother for sixteen years, never gets birthday or Christmas cards from her, never sends her any either, hates her passionately and loves her still.

Having felt his eyelids grow unbearably heavy and his head fill with lead an hour ago, but having resisted it for all this time so he could get the prologue to his story told, the Rugged Man suddenly succumbs mid-sentence to sleep. As his soft palate loosens and his mouth falls open, a gentle snore ebbs and flows through the room. Nearly drifting off myself to soak in that blessed balm of hurt minds, I think I should probably go home now. I think I should rouse myself and slip quietly out the door and hope I might run into him again sometime, somewhere down the track. But I stay on the armchair for a little while longer. I light a cigarette, kick-start it with a deep inhale, put the ashtray on the table next to me, sit back and chill out. And watch.

I watch him sleep. As the protective layers of masks kept in place by wary consciousness begin to lift off and fall away, I see the soft edge of his true face settle into shape underneath. I watch as a drizzle of dribble dampens the cushion that his head rests on. I watch as his slackened mouth moves with a soundless proclamation of some adamant sort to some unseen one. I watch as his fists clench and his arm twitches and a tremor runs down his leg as he encounters whatever demons lurk in his dreamtime. And I watch as the little lost child within him rises brave and vulnerable and full of dread to see if he can survive yet another round of dark and disturbance and phantoms and fear and all the agitated perils that pervade in his night.

Twenty-eight

As I watch him, I feel a magnetic pull strengthen between us. It intensifies the longer I hold my look, until its insistence is too strong to ignore. It urges me to go to him and lay beside him and sink into his body and pull his arms around me. It impels me to look closely at this Rugged Man, to see how our forms fit, to recognise the drive that draws us together. My whining heart wants to leave now but I, unable to resist this force any longer, move to where he is asleep on the couch.

I kneel down on the floor in line with his chest. The magnetic pull is in full flight now. And I suddenly see, with a blinding burst of absolute understanding, the silent shadowy hues of his heart. Like mine, it resolutely hides from view and has its back turned to the world. Like mine, it carries rips and tears and wounds and scars. Like mine, it has long since refused to be open and has shut itself up tight and firmly fixed the closed sign in place. Like mine, it is shrivelled and pea-sized and hardened and hopeless.

Like mine, it is, so much like mine. I see now why I am here, where I belong and what I am destined for. I see now who this Rugged Man really is, the exact match for my messed-up heart. She might disagree and want to run, but I see now that here, with this Rugged Man, I have found my dark and dusty little corner of the world, a place where I fit, where I can simply be my worn-down self, where my heart can take whatever distorted shape she likes. I have found the one that is more my kind, a little beaten, a little blue, a little bent, he is, my Rugged Man.

*

It never ceases to amaze me how much crap I have accumulated over a short span of time with virtually no money. Just like my mother. Not dust-collecting trinkets so much as handbags and heels and hand-me-down accessories. What was another woman's trash became my valued treasure until I decided to move in with my Rugged Man and realised it was actually trash after all. And now I have to wade through raging rivers of it. Clearing out the seemingly endless rows of shoved-away rubbish at the back of my wardrobe, I come across the green-and-white-striped shoe box I hid there years ago. I know what is in it and there is no way, right now, and probably for a long time, I will open it to remind myself. I place it carefully in a packing box and cover it gently with butcher's paper so it can be safe.

Behind another pile of hideous charity-store heels lies a mysterious, taped-up, vanilla cardboard folder. I cut open the package and try to contain

Twenty-eight

the yellowing pages of handwritten print that fall out. I recognise the words as the only manuscript I have actually finished, a year after university, still in the naive throes of hope that something I write might actually find a publisher. Until my apparent best friend Fiona read it. Everyone knew she was our year's most promising graduate, gifted, a natural, the next big thing in literature. And strangely, she was my friend. Fiona was ever encouraging, plucked those long forgotten strings inside me that yearned to pick out a story, promised me I could win after all. And I wrote that story, start to finish, and put it in her hands before putting it in the post. It came back, marked and crossed, scribbled on and scrawled over. She hated it. I grew to hate it too.

Of course, Fiona was going to let me read her manuscript but was too eager to let it set sail. And sail it did, right into the most magnificent sunset you could ever imagine. Publishing war, awards galore, overseas editions, worldwide acclaim. She flicked me off like a biting fire ant and ran off into a fabulous future of fame and much cooler friends. I dusted myself off, taped up my crap manuscript, chucked it in the back of the wardrobe and vowed to keep all supposed friends at a distance. Luckily my Rugged Man feels no need for them either. We both agree there are too many people in the world and we would rather not get to know any of them. We have each other, and that is enough. I throw the yellowed pages onto the rubbish heap.

Back on the climbing chair, I reach for the final grimy remnants of my wardrobe relics and the last thing I pull out looks to be an old rolled-up poster, covered in brown paper and tied with a red ribbon. It takes me a full five minutes to remember where it came from. Mum, Christmas, seven years ago, to put in a special place to look at when I am feeling low, the light bulb goes on. Considering what had happened later that fateful Christmas Day and over the course of that fearsome following week, I had forgotten all about this strange little present Mum was so particular about.

In a surge of curious anticipation, I pull the ribbon off and rip away the brown paper. The old poster unravels quickly to reveal a jarring image in front of me, hurtling me back through time to my childhood delirium. An electric jolt sears my heart as I remember. Me, small, covered in gold and white sparkling paint, pleased as punch, muttering to myself, fixing a tiny gold shape of a love heart to the centre of this crazy finger painting and imagining how extraordinary I will look in Miss Blossom's dance routine, dressed as the beautiful Astintina.

Twenty-eight

Rigid, I stare at it. Why has Mum kept this ludicrous finger painting all these years? Thinking it would make me happy, thinking it would make me smile, maybe laugh, maybe want to reminisce about that time? I hated those years. I can barely look at it. I just shake my head, over and over, an annoyed glitch repeating through my system, trying to settle down the agitated jitterbug jumping through my veins. My heart, typically, has gone into a baffled hopeful spasm thinking she has received a sudden bolt of lightning from Astintina's heart like in the old days. And she cannot help herself, cannot resist a chance to flash a spiteful image through my mind of that recurring nightmare I had years ago, of waking on a cold slab with her nearly dying, and Astintina alongside my Beautiful Man trying to revive me.

A Beautiful Man, he was, but not mine. I remind myself and my heart, he was not ours.

Yet still I shake inexplicably, a torturous feeling of a hundred knives stabbing through every inch of my flesh. I command myself to assume some control. I throw the stupid painting on the heap of crap marked for the trash. I light a cigarette quickly and warn my pathetic heart to stop her spasms immediately. I tell my body to pull itself together and stop jerking around like a mad marionette getting machine-gunned. And I order my mind to get a grip on itself and stop taking me back to an age best forgotten. I tell myself sternly, all of that is dead and buried, a whole other world sunk at sea, one I could never have found a home in anyway. I suck on my cigarette like it is my very own thumb and I am a hungry baby again.

Slowly, as the nicotine rushes to every end of every capillary in every part of my body, infusing my blood with much-needed, numbing medicine, I begin to come back to my senses. I start to laugh. Clearly, I have lost more than a healthy number of brain cells over the years to react in such a way. Obviously, my nerves are fraying with this important move to freak out so suddenly like that. Perhaps, this is a bigger deal than I first thought, moving in with my Rugged Man, embarking on a new life together, making the sort of commitment I never thought I would, making a home that I hope will sustain us through the years. My hermit heart makes no bones about what she thinks. A mistake, she weakly thumps. But I have done it now and there is no turning back. Onwards and upwards, I write in my cheap and battered diary.

Onwards and upwards, come what may.

Rolling it up without looking at it again, I put the finger painting poster in my suitcase. I decide

Twenty-eight

not to throw it out just yet. It is quite funny after all. My Rugged Man will think it hysterical. Maybe the next time I open it, a little way down the track, it will give me the good laugh it should.

*

A piercing crack of sunlight is stabbing straight through my left eye socket and carving up my brain. My Rugged Man lies catatonic next to me, immune to the disease of daylight spreading through the room. It is two in the afternoon and I promised myself, as a new-house and new-life resolution, I would get in at least an hour of writing before my paid work of waitressing begins. I roll over to give the sleeping him a final embrace and realise it would take more willpower than the whole world could muster to lift me out of a man's warm, wrapped-around-me arms.

Instead, I lay back and I think about what I will write when I make myself get up tomorrow. Tucked away in my bottom drawer are the several first beginnings of stories to work with. I have many different genres to choose from. I could persevere with the futuristic science-fiction fantasy or thrust ahead on the thinking woman's broadly historical bodice ripper. I have four solid pages of a potential ripsnorter about a clairvoyant archaeologist searching for the lost city of Atlantis or perhaps I should focus on my reasonably detailed outline of a children's tale of tolerance involving a bilby and a blue-tongue lizard.

In an attempt to avoid exhibiting the loathsome laziness that foretells a total failure, I pull out my new diary, hard-covered and crisp and coloured with roses, a house-warming present from my Rugged Man. I look at him and the home we are making and write about where we are at. The new apartment is small and the walls need a paint, but we are making it cosy and it works for now. While he uses almost every saucepan in the house making dinner and has never heard of the phrase 'clean up as you go', my Rugged Man is a wonderful cook, coming up with the most interesting flavours. Even though the rent seems high and we have already received several overdue bill notices and we do not always agree on each other's spending habits, we have only fought over money twice.

And as we walked home after work, in the deep dark middle of last night, with the shadows swirling and spitting around us, he linked his arm through mine. And amidst the sounds of fights breaking out and bottles smashing and drunken idiots yelling, he held my hand tight. And when lewd gestures were made and dirty remarks came our way, he fixed the

Twenty-eight

culprits with a killer stare and they collapsed like a spineless house of cards on the spot. And for the first time in what felt like forever, I had a Night of the Long Walks Home with no fear.

With my Rugged Man by my side, I felt no sickening cringe in my gut at what lurked round the next corner. My keys stayed untouched in my handbag and my fingers stayed loose and open in his. I had no need for weak weapons and fists and fierce thoughts. No need to rally my pitiful courage at creeping post boxes. For the first time in what felt like forever, I walked with an air of strength, of power, of protection, wrapped up in my Rugged Man's force-field of safety.

And while I still like to keep my steak knife in the pillowcase, for a little comfort, just in case, I know I will never need it when my Rugged Man's around.

*

Nervous excitement scampers about our little apartment this morning. We are both washing and shaving and primping and preening and making sure we put on our Sunday best. For today, my Rugged Man has a very important audition and I have a very important job interview. The planets have aligned and the stars have united and the universe is set to provide and this day will be known as the turning of the tide on which both our ships come in.

Clutching a scrappy bitser book of a hotchpotch portfolio containing my every tiny piece of published nonsense, I can barely endure the agonisingly long wait to be seen. Each minute is a monstrosity of angst and insecurity as I watch a parade of flawless fashionista women, oozing feline assurance and covert killer instincts, come and go through the interview-room door. Some of them flash a smile at me and I see shades of Fiona lurking in their hearts. Most of them sit several classes above me and it is all I can do to not sink deep into the leathery armchair, in a sea of my own sweat and tears, and silently drown.

I am called in. An impossibly immaculate, silver-haired, Chanel-suited, spine-chilling Succubus stalks me with her icy eyes as I slink into the room and promptly trip on her plump Persian rug.

Oh my god, I am so sorry... I am so clumsy sometimes.

I pick myself up and sit down to terrorising silence.

That is a lovely rug though, by the way... very thick, very... lovely.

The Succubus just stares at me, a stare weighted with a thousand Samurai swords slicing me into millions of miniscule pieces. I gabber on.

Twenty-eight

Um, I am just so . . . really pleased that you, that I actually got this . . . um, to have this face to face with you. It really does mean a lot.

The Succubus holds out her delicate hand, encrusted with half the world's quota of probably blood diamonds and I rise up to shake it. She stops me.

The portfolio.

Oh, yes . . . sorry . . . of course.

The Succubus turns each page with an achingly slow, swelling disdain.

Um, you'll see that there probably isn't much there that, um . . . that you can really get an idea of what I can do, you know . . . it can be quite hard to, you know, get stuff out there, but . . . which is why this is so great, you know . . . it's something I would really love to try, to, you know . . . be a part of, this magazine thing, this whole world of . . . researching for and . . . you know, one day, maybe, writing for the magazine.

The Succubus secretes a weary and wintry sigh, then speaks.

Understand this. You will not be employed for your clever wordsmithery, your cunning wit, your undiscovered talent. You are here to be a mere galley slave in my empire and you will do as you are told. Remember, you are the least impressive of the applicants for this job by a long shot and that is why you have the position. I am not interested in someone who harbours great ambitions.

My heart squeaks a whimper, but I recover quickly.

Well, that's ... definitely me, I don't harbour any ... I really don't.

Good. You start in two weeks.

The Succubus nods to the door and I crawl away, clutching my tail tightly between my legs.

It's true, I remind my disappointed, delusional heart. I do not harbour any great ambition. I do not have the drive needed to make a masterpiece. I struggle to get out of bed in the morning. My grand plans for a Great Life Purpose were extinguished long ago. And now, luckily, here I am, the least impressive applicant for the position. And, because of that, I got the job. I will be a writer of sorts after all.

*

As my Rugged Man and I get spruced up for some sort of farewell party from my shitful function waitressing life, he finally gets the phone call he has been waiting for on tenterhooks all week from his acting agent. He breathes deep, wipes his sweaty palms, wears a facade of faux gusto and goes into the other room to answer the phone.

Twenty-eight

Hey, hey, what's the story?

My ears stretch out and start to ache trying to hear the outcome. Silence, a murmur, silence, a grunt.

Too old? . . . Right, well, I thought the character was mid-thirties . . . well, okay then, it'll be interesting to see who they go with . . . yeah, okay, thanks . . . yeah, for sure.

He hangs up the phone. Silence. I wait, my stomach sinking for him. It is a full three minutes before my Rugged Man comes back into the bedroom.

Didn't get the part.

Oh, baby.

Fuckers. They reckon it's an age thing but I bet my bottom dollar it's what's-his-face who used to be the floor manager when I was on that TV show. He hated me then, and now he's calling the bloody shots. No wonder I can't get arrested with that bloody network. It's gotta be him. Fucking arsehole.

His hands shake like a mini earthquake erupting as he lights a cigarette.

Shit script anyway.

The dark mist circling my Rugged Man's head grows thicker and heavier as the night wears on. It soon morphs into a brutal, black cloud threatening to burst forth thunder and hail and lightning strikes at any moment. Fed by hard liquor, hothouse marijuana and several lines of south-of-the-border coke, this monstrous gathering storm soon engulfs his whole being. As the night draws to a close, I wonder when and how this maelstrom will be unleashed.

It breaks the second we enter the bedroom. He turns to me with an overcast, dark, macabre light in his eyes, irrational eyes that seem to be completely severed from the mind that animates them. I wonder where his mind has gone and if I will be able to get it back. My heart begins to flutter in anxious anticipation. The room is turning shivering cold with the icy insanity in the air. He grabs my arm and holds it firm and fixes me with a freezing glare. The squall begins.

I guess you think that was okay, do you?
What?
Guess you thought you'd just have, what, a bit of fun, hey?
I'm not sure—
At my expense.
What d'you mean?
You're completely oblivious, aren't you?
I don't—
Completely fucking oblivious.
If you'd just tell me—
You know what you were doing! You fucking

Twenty-eight

know! In front of everyone. Like a fucking wanna-be strip-club dancer, all over that fucking poof, in front of everyone!

Who, Simon?

Yeah, fucking simple Simon, you know who I mean.

He's gay!

So?

So, I wasn't like, trying to—

You're that fucking thick, are you? You stupid bitch. Gyrating away, thrusting your fucking tits in his face and your cunt at his cock, you don't think every other fucking cock spank in that club was staring at you and wanting a piece of it. There's me, your little cock-on-a-tie, at the bar, getting you a drink, I turn around and you're acting like a fucking slut who doesn't get enough.

I was just having a dance!

Oh fuck off, I'm not a fucking idiot! D'you think I'm a fucking idiot?!

No, of course—

So stop fucking treating me like one! If you're not happy here then fuck off.

I am happy here!

Then what, you're not getting enough of it, hey? Is that it?

Roaring to prove a sadistic point, he tears off his

jacket and shirt and pushes me down on the bed. My terrified heart begins to quake wildly, sending erratic beats and congealing blood through my brain and I lose all control of my limbs as they start convulsing with grand mal confusion.

How about this then, hey? I'll give you a good fuck, hey?

No baby, not like this—

Fucking no? No? After you've been gagging for it all night. Or what, you don't want it from me, is that it?

No, I—

Is that fucking it?

He rips my knickers off and unbuckles his jeans. He pulls out his dick and starts yanking it up and down. It stays resolutely flaccid.

C'mon baby, we've both had too much to drink.

I try to get up and he pushes me back down.

Just you fucking wait!

A giggle of fear, of panic, of self-conscious fright bubbles up uncontrollably from my belly and bursts out of my mouth as a laugh.

You're not gonna get it up baby.

DON'T YOU DARE FUCKING LAUGH AT ME!

In what seems like agonisingly slow motion, my Rugged Man's eyes flash with humiliated madness, his heart flushes black, his hand rises up. I try to

Twenty-eight

move out of the way, his hand comes crashing down with full force onto the side of my face.

For a split second I lose consciousness and see the bright white body of Astintina, so brilliant my mind stings. Then, I ricochet back into my thumping body and taste the bitter metallic blood in my mouth. My eyes are bulging, my ears are screaming, my teeth are throbbing. My brain is fried numb into an electric shock stupor. My heart is constricted and shockingly silent. For a moment I think she has stopped. Then a tremor of loathing waves through her once.

*

As he sleeps, catatonic on the couch, I gulp down four pain-killers and ice my swelling face. I fire up a joint, fat and toxic, and hold back the waves of sickness long enough to sink into a soporific fog of forgetting everything.

In another plane of consciousness, I am swimming lazily, an easy freestyle, over long languid laps, back and forth. Little by little, I feel the lactic acid build up and burn my now bruising body so I turn my final roll and head down to the deep end of the pool for my last lap. Suddenly, I see them. Sinister, malevolent, evil, enormous, six Great White Pointer Sharks gliding patiently along the bottom, waiting for a swimmer to stop and sink so they can strike. As one of these monsters meets my eye, I lose control of my bladder and the scented spiral of my urine drifts down to their beady, greedy senses and they lap it up. They accelerate their circling, lascivious and salivating, knowing the arrival of their next feast is imminent.

It is not long before exhaustion has transformed the blood in my body to liquid lead and my bones into rods of iron, which rip up and waste away my muscles with their weight. I know I cannot last much longer. I do not see the point of trying to last much longer. I know I cannot escape my miserable Fate. And so I surrender. As I sink, stiff, paralysed with dread, I see the serrated jaws of my gruesome death drooling in voracious anticipation of eating me alive.

I wake up bolt upright. Breathless, sweating, my underwear soiled, grasping the telephone. In my feverish state, I have begun to dial Dad's number. I think of when he held me before he left with my heart dancing zealously in his hands and my desperate self sure we had a chance. I wish I could go back to that time, to try again, to try harder, to try and send my destiny off on a better track. I hang up the phone. And I let the dam burst. Shaking, gasping, sobbing, swaying, weeping, spluttering, the whole catastrophe.

My Rugged Man must have heard me because the next thing I know, he is rocking me in his arms, like

Twenty-eight

a precious baby in a penitent cradle. He is crying too, stammering, gulping, whispering his sorry over and over. He tells me that he does not know what came over him, that something within him snapped, that the drink and the drugs made him lose his mind. He begs me to forgive him, to let him start over, to let him make it up to me. He promises it will never happen again, that he will take care of me, that I can trust him. He confesses to me that he is ashamed of himself, that he hates himself deeply, that he cannot believe I could love him.

I tell him I understand. And I do. Even though my ever-blackening heart disagrees, I know it is these very things that have taken virulent root inside of me and grow bigger and stronger every day in my gut. The same shame, the same self-hatred, the same disbelief someone could love me. And the deep bottomless pit of fear that they will leave.

I tell him I love him and that I will stay.

*

I hide inside over the next few days, waiting for the swelling in my face to subside. Restless, with yet another icepack on my face, I call Mum.

Hey, it's me.
Hey love . . . is everything all right?
Yeah, of course, why wouldn't it be?

Well, nothing, it's just that . . . you only called me the other day, about your job.

Oh, well, can't I call my mother when I want?

Don't be silly, you know you can.

Well, good.

Have you started work yet?

In a week.

I'm so happy for you, love.

Thanks Mum.

I just hated the thought of you having to do all that waitressing.

Mmmm.

It can be so hard on your feet.

Yeah . . . so, how are things with you?

Oh, you know, good . . . same as usual.

You getting out much?

Oh, you know . . . did you see that lady on Oprah?

Um, no.

The one that had that acid thrown at her?

No, but doesn't sound good.

No, horrible, horrible story . . . got me a bit teary, it did.

Well . . . don't go getting all stressed about it.

You should put that sort of stuff in your magazine.

People don't really want to hear that sort of stuff, Mum, . . . it's quite depressing.

You're probably right.

Twenty-eight

You taking all your tablets?

No, I'm flushing them down the toilet, what d'you think?

Geez, just asking . . . don't have to get defensive.

What's wrong with your voice?

Nothing.

It sounds funny.

Does it?

I move the icepack off my cheek.

How's that?

That's better.

I was holding the phone funny.

Are you sure everything's all right, love?

For a moment I think about telling her the truth. How my face aches and my body is tired and I find it hard to get up in the mornings. I think about asking her to come and pick me up and take me home and help me start all over again. Then I remember her wasted-away and worrying heart and how much of a burden I have already been to it. I take a deep breath and infuse the biggest smile I can through my voice.

Everything's great Mum, don't you worry.

That afternoon, I go to the top of my side of the wardrobe and pull out the green-and-white-striped shoe box tucked away at the very back. I think I am numb enough now to open it. I do not touch those precious things kept inside, just stare at them and absorb their loveliness. The now written-in, beautifully bound in soft leather, faded burgundy writing book held closed by a delicate bronze butterfly. The breathtakingly exquisite turquoise and silver pendant that may be powerfully healing, though I have never tried to wear it and find out. The cute-as-pie, rascal of a raggedy teddy bear which stares back at me with deep, black eyes.

And then, in the corner of the shoe box, the glimmering golden trinket box I do not dare to open. I remember vividly its contents, though, a magical enchantment of a charm bracelet, twinkling with a universe of suns and moons and stars and magic. And the memory is enough. There was such joy in my life for a moment and that is more than I thought I would ever have. I close the lid and push the box back into its hiding place.

*

Life always seems to be able to go on regardless. My Rugged Man is on his best behaviour, reminding me of the goodness and tenderness at the core of him, alongside the delicate daily pain of his wounds that may never heal and I know we fit so well together. My new job is a snake pit of ambition and treachery but no one thinks too much of me so I am safe there for the moment.

Twenty-eight

And I am not really surprised at the stony walls of silence surrounding my heart these days. After the incident, she seemed to slow right down and slip away into the distance. It is almost like she removed herself physically from me. And as each day passes, I learn to embrace her seeming absence and not rally so hard against the numbness spreading through my chest. I learn to accept the anaesthetised comfort of this feeling I now have, of a sort of emptiness, a nothingness, a void. The feeling of being, very nearly, heartless.

thirty-five

For the past ten minutes I have been slowly hypnotised by a ghastly black, hairy and lopsided seven-legged spider hanging two feet in front of my face. It is the size of a small dog, seems to be made out of chewed-up ice-cream sticks and recycled pipe cleaners and has what appears to be three eyes that stare straight at me as it dangles back and forth on an occasional draught. Other bugs of other kinds, from stink beetles to ladybirds to stick insects, swing down seductively from the roof, but it is my endearingly ogreish spider that has steadfastly distracted me from taking any halfway decent notes on the Al-Anon meeting I am attending. I wonder whose idea it was to hold this very serious discussion in the rather frolicsome setting of a Steiner primary school.

As living proof of the old saying 'beware the quiet ones', I have recently been appointed subeditor of my magazine. While everyone else was busily beefing up their career achievements, stabbing everyone else in the back and big-noting themselves to the Succubus, I knew the real secret to ladder-climbing success. Never appear to be a threat, real or otherwise. Do whatever the Succubus says, whenever she says it, with passable competence and barely any panache and she will hiss at you, tell you she detests your writing, change three words in your article, claim it as her own, and clutch you even closer as you continue to make her look positively brilliant.

And I have long since learnt to ignore the fragments of whispered conversation from the staffroom that travel effortlessly next door and straight into my office without anyone knowing.

So, looks like the teacher's pet got that promotion again.

That's 'cos her head's so far up the Succubus' arse she's tickling her tonsils with her tongue.

There's something sick about the two of them together, like a dominatrix and her gimp.

D'you think they're on together?

No, dickhead, she's with that actor who used to be on that show.

Which one?

Thirty-five

Oh, that one with, you know . . .

I could never imagine her with, like . . . she's just so uptight and so, I don't know . . . organised. And bossy.

She probably makes him schedule in sex time.

I so do not want to think about her having sex.

She's not that bad-looking.

I know, but, you know, she's so, like, cold, reptilian, it'd be like doing it with a dead komodo dragon.

That's so gross!

Don't you think she's kind of weirdly matronly too . . . like this freaky nun that I had in high school.

Hey, have you ever noticed those bruises?

What bruises?

Like, on her legs.

Yeah, you wouldn't pick her as being clumsy.

And I've seen some weird ones around her wrists.

Oooh, kinky.

And remember when she had those days off with the flu, she came back with a sort of old bruise near her left eye, remember?

She does always wear a lot of make-up.

Don't you think that's suss?

What, d'you think he's like . . . ?

Maybe.

No!

I'm sorry but I just cannot see our so-in-control-I'm-God subeditor copping it at home.

Yeah, she'd be the type to hit him back even harder.

Yeah, you're right, you would not want to mess with her.

Oh, shit, that reminds me, I'm supposed to have that stupid diet story finished by four!

Oh, dear, you're guts for garters, honey.

Even though my heart squeezes into an even tighter ball of shame when she hears these barbed words, I have learnt to steel myself against their cuts. I have no time for the saga and gossip and game-playing of so-called friends. Trust is hard won and not a single person in this building would have the metal needed to fight for it.

Generally, in my position as subeditor, I would not be called upon to attend something like an Al-Anon meeting. Mercifully, I usually would not have to go anywhere near the tedious writing of these so-called meaningful stories that are designed to make the magazine look less tabloid. The Succubus insists on peppering her weekly trash with the occasional inspirational story of one woman's courageous crusade against all odds. This is the singular sorry attempt at nourishing a near-extinct female sense of self-esteem, in between reams of pages dedicated to ridiculing as many other women as possible, humiliating any celebrity with cellulite and ordering each

Thirty-five

and every woman who wants to get ahead to stock up on expensive cosmetics, skimpy dresses and the latest in scam fitness equipment. Today, the brave battle of our hero woman centres around her life with an alcoholic, hence the Al-Anon meeting and my subsequent cursing of the feature writer who would ordinarily be doing this, but who cunningly orchestrated her water breaking and a twenty-two-hour labour earlier in the week.

I force myself to stop fixating on the spider and direct my attention to the softly spoken fifteen-year-old girl holding centre stage. She talks about her mother's all-night bender over the weekend and having to clean her vomit off their couch so the girl and her younger brother could watch television. I stifle a grimace as I remember my Rugged Man's epic vomiting session in the bath three weeks ago after he had failed to get yet another much-desired acting job. The seriously putrid spew was five centimetres deep in places and he had charmingly collapsed with his left arm dangling in it.

Next up is a bleached-blonde, gum-chewing young woman on crutches who confesses she is a recovering alcoholic living with her in-denial alcoholic husband. Referring to her crutches, she tells us her husband, in a violent fit of alcohol-induced rage, ran her over when she got out of the car during a fight last week. As she lists all the other things that have happened over the last month, from broken ribs to busted eardrums to boiling water poured over her back, I thank the heavens that the fights I have with my Rugged Man are tame in comparison. While he has broken my ribs a few times, given me the odd black eye and scared the living daylights out of me, he has never burnt me or run me over or put me in the hospital, the whole seven years we have been together.

As I look with disdainful pity at this young woman and wonder how on earth she could stay with her ultra-violent husband, I catch a quick glimpse of her hidden-away heart. It is tiny and timid and a tattered mess, worm-holed and worn and pale red from over-bleeding. I looked around the group and see that most of their hearts, though they are careful to keep them cleverly concealed, are all in some similar state of devastation and disrepair.

Only one person has her heart on display. She sits at the head of the table and seems to be the unspoken coordinator of the proceedings. She must be pushing sixty because her hair is unashamedly grey, her brow embedded with creases and her shoulders a little stooped from carrying, presumably, an uneasy burden over endless miles of rocky roads. Still, her heart sits serene on her sleeve. Sporting the shadows

Thirty-five

of war wounds and battle scars, it seems to have found succour in some magic elixir of something along the way, some strength or hope or faith or courage, something with the power to pull a weary heart through. I lean slightly forward to make sure I hear her secrets.

It seems she has been going to Al-Anon meetings for twenty-seven years. She remembers an old man at her very first meeting, with a young light in his eyes talking about making lists. My ears prick up at this because I am an exceptionally fastidious, passionately committed and profoundly true convert to the magical art of list making. My entire life is a series of completed lists. Apart from the list of stories I want to write – I am saving that list for when I have time in my dotage – every step of my every day is completing the next item on my current list. I excitedly pick up my pen to scribble down the old woman's recounting of the even older man's wise words on making lists.

He said . . . Hear you this. There is one list that I challenge you to make. Without a doubt, it will be a difficult journey that, once made, will be a blinding revelation. Make this list, then live this list and freedom will be yours. This list must comprise twenty things . . .

The old woman pauses for maximum effect and

I almost have to wipe the drool that is threatening to dribble from my mouth, but I manage to suck it back up in time.

The twenty things in your life that bring you joy.

And that's it. That's the supposedly life-changing list. Knock me down with a feather. With that, the meeting is over and I walk out with raised eyebrows. While my near-paralysed heart has managed a half-hearted twirl at the talk of the list, I am thoroughly unimpressed. Even riding on the eager steam of my passionate love of list making, that suggestion is a dismal disappointment, a miserable anti-climax. In fact, the whole meeting lacks inspiration. Staring at my measly notes, I wonder how I am ever going to cook up some rousing crowd-stirrer of a story for our tabloid magazine. Curse the maternity leavers and their long, painful labours.

Late that night, after a nonsensical dream about an endless shopping list and women stabbing each other over it at an End-of-Year Stocktake Sale, I decide to write a heading in my shiny black recycled paper diary. 'Twenty Things in My Life That Bring Me Joy'. I promise myself I will finish it off tomorrow, then double-check my steak knife is in position and snuggle back up to my warm Rugged Man in bed.

*

Thirty-five

Sucking back on an essential evening sedative of a spliff, while the television flashes a hypnotic series of mindless scenes before me, is my near-perfect way to end a day. For the most part, my Rugged Man and I will drift off into our own soporific worlds, barely saying anything to each other, but enjoying the primal comfort of another body nearby. These nights, as the drug soothes the heat that steams up from his soul, my Rugged Man relaxes, cools calmly down and quietly relishes the welcome amnesia that softly washes over his troubled mind and taunted heart. These nights, without the dread of a possible uprising from his destructive rage, I too can allow the drug to loosen my restless, strung-out-on-razor-wire nerves, free the fraying fibres in my rigid muscles and ease the anxiety that oozes relentlessly from my apprehensive heart.

On other rare and wonderful nights, one of us will experience a bolt of lucid lightning to the brain and burst forth with a brilliant idea. In the convoluted, THC-intoxicated retelling of this mind-blowing epiphany, the listener will invariably seize up with snorting laughter and spark a similar fit of hysterics in the other. Back and forth we go in a hailstorm of hilarity that leaves us both in happily sore stitches. Tonight, I have one such genius brainwave.

Oh my god . . . I have just thought of a brilliant idea

for a book! Oh my god ... okay so, right ... the story starts at a funeral and there's this guy giving a eulogy. Except he keeps referring to himself in it and we realise that it's actually his very own funeral. So, okay, the minute he finishes the eulogy he just, suddenly, dies ... he just, internally combusts on the spot ... you know, with just his, maybe, shoes left behind ... and while everyone's naturally sad, everyone is also really happy that this guy got to choose when he was going to die. Because, you see, there is this group of spiritualists, right, who have been teaching people how they can essentially euthanase themselves ... by consciously willing the body to actually self-destruct. And this course has been so successful that the government ... it's set in the future, right ... has outlawed the group because so many people have been choosing to die ... left, right and centre, they're doing it, dying at their own funerals. So it becomes this story about ... a quest, if you will, for the right to, you know, euthanase yourself ... to be able to choose when you can die and, you know, plan for it ... to even be at your own funeral, and let it be this real celebration of your life, and everything.

A long and silent pause.

What d'you think?

My Rugged Man stifles a smirk.

They internally combust on the spot ... at their own funeral?

Thirty-five

Yeah, you know . . . after they give their eulogy.
Leaving behind their shoes?
Yeah, possibly, it could be kind of symbolic.
Right.
So, what d'you think?

My Rugged Man cannot hold it back any longer. He starts to choke up, snorting and grunting, stifling his amusement for as long as he can whilst trying to speak.

Internally . . . combust . . . on the . . . spot!

And the laughter bursts open, surging out, roaring and chortling, drenching everything in its path.

My god, you come up with some crap . . . no wonder you've never finished anything.

Even though my heart stings with his words, I ignore her and let myself get swept up with his jesting and we both laugh our insides out for the next half an hour over the sheer absurdity of the idea. I tell myself it really was meant to be a joke even though I know, when I first thought it, I was deadly serious. All is well when my Rugged Man and I laugh together, play together, when we connect over something lighter, something happier, something pointedly different from our mutual pain. These are my favourite nights.

Tonight, in the dying waves of this revelry, the

phone rings. I pull myself together, kiss my Rugged Man on the lips and ruffle his hair, then answer it.

Hello, love.

Dad?!

Yeah, look, just a quick call, we're in town and we wanted to know if you want to meet up on Saturday.

You're here in the city?

Yeah, we're having lunch for your sister's twenty-first and since she's here at the uni, we thought we'd come in.

She's at the uni?

Yeah, you know, she's doing some Arts and Law degree or something at that place near the racecourse, you know the one.

Yeah, I know the one.

Yeah, she's doing really well, nearly top of her class, she'll be graduating at the end of the year.

Right . . . that's nice.

So, we thought we might as well have this lunch.

For sure.

And she said it'd be good if you could come.

Oh, okay . . . right.

So, you'll come?

Um . . . yeah, sure . . . why not.

My heart keeps stammering a syncopated staccato beat as I throw handful after handful of chillingly cold water on my face. My head is

Thirty-five

spinning and my legs are shaking and I cling to the sides of the basin to stay upright. My stepsister is turning twenty-one. That favourite little baby with the perfect pretty heart. The one that I held in my arms for so many of those fearsome photos. The one that I imagined at the bottom of the cliffs with its brains dashed out. The one I would watch with my dad in the shower as I felt my whole being flush green with envy. The one who is now all grown up and studying at the same university I did. The one who wants me to be at her celebratory lunch on Saturday. The one who, after all these years, is now about to turn twenty-one. Has it really been that long?

I stare at myself in the mirror. I see with brutal clarity every line, wrinkle, scar, spot, crease and crinkle that callous Time has hammered into my face. I see how awfully old I have become in those twenty-one years. I see the weariness, the haggardness, the sallowness, not simply in my flesh but in my very soul. I see the limping older woman that the little girl dancing as Astintina has grown into. What I would not give to have my very own picture of Dorian Gray hiding in my attic, harbouring all my rank and rotten etchings of experience on its face, so that I could walk fraudulently tall in the sunlight, sit smiling and luminous at that lunch, conceal any trace of my true heartache, and deceive all with my striking semblance of beauty.

What I would not give.

*

It was the Friday night before the Saturday lunch and nothing was going my way. First, I was running repulsively late at work with deadlines threatening to be missed and the Succubus menacing me with her reptilian wrath. Then, the crawling traffic was unbearably choking at every turn and it was all I could do to stop the top of my head from exploding with the volcano of road rage building inside me. So, by the time I got home, it was a long way past dinnertime and the cheap Chinese takeaway I had rummaged up two hours ago was cold and congealed in its leaking plastic container. My Rugged Man was not at home and from past experience, I knew this was not a good sign. I ate barely a few mouthfuls of my portion of beef and black bean before my troubled belly blew it all back out of my mouth.

Inevitably, my Rugged Man came home pissed and picking a fight, having been up at the pub washing down his sinewy steak sandwich with several schooners of second-rate beer. In a predictable old routine, he sneered at the terrible takeaway,

Thirty-five

grabbed my arms in a vice-like grip, seemed about to shove my face in the food, then pushed me to the floor instead, and threw the beef and black bean against the wall. After a barrage of insults and invectives, spitting and swearing, fist thumping and foot stamping, the hurricane suddenly ran out of wind, he shook his head in disgust and marched off to the bedroom.

Relieved at the relative lightness of the argument, I picked myself up off the floor and headed into the kitchen to collect myself over a cup of tea. I certainly did not fancy going into the bedroom to kiss and make up with him just yet. I breathed in cautiously, felt that familiar stabbing sensation in my back and knew that I had put out a rib. My arms were throbbing with a recognisable ache and I knew several bruises would definitely show up by tomorrow. I had wanted to wear my new, white-with-red-roses-patterned summer dress at lunch, but it was short-sleeved. For some bizarre reason, floral patterns were one of the few things that had the power to make me feel somewhat feminine at the moment, so I decided to go back to the store in the morning and see if I could find a similar alternative with sufficient arm covering.

Standing next to a copy of my white-with-red-roses dress in the store the next day, I called over the heavily made-up, synthetic-cleavaged and enormous-earring-wearing teenager apparently running the store.

I need this in long sleeves.

It's, like, a summer dress.

Right, well . . . I need it with long sleeves.

Summer dresses are, like, made for summer so they have, like, you know, no sleeves.

Well, I'm looking for a summer dress with long sleeves, if that's all right.

But it's, like, summer . . . you are going to, like, boil.

I doubt that.

But aren't you, like, boiling right now in that cardigan?

Not at all.

Well, no one I know wears long sleeves in summer.

Well, I do, if that's all right with you, so do you have a dress with long sleeves or not . . . please?

Well, not . . . no.

Nothing?

It's summer.

Oh for god's sake.

I huffed out of the store, hopped with indignation into my compact little beep of a car and started the engine as fast as I could to fire up the airconditioning full blast. It was the height of summer and

Thirty-five

it was actually very hot and this damned cardigan was a veritable furnace. But there was no way I was going to take it off. I looked at myself in the mirror. I was sweating, my face was flushed red, my mascara was bleeding and my make-up was virtually sliding off my face. The lunch was in fifteen minutes.

Even though frustrated sobs were rising fast in my throat, I swallowed them down with a determined splutter. I drove to the restaurant where lunch was being held and parked the car close by. As I was about to step out onto the street, I saw my dad cross the road, holding the hand of a beautiful young woman. She stood tall and self-possessed, strong and self-assured. Other people could not help but look at her as they passed by, admiring this sweet specimen of a lovely young lady. Dad was clearly proud, his attention fixed on her, his smile affirming her favoured position. And she was happily gracious in the knowledge that the world lay adoring at her feet. Today, she knew that she was standing at her adult threshold, the door to the rest of her wondrous life beckoning. And today, now twenty-one, she finally held the castle key that would open it all wide and ripe before her.

How I envied her. To be twenty-one again. Knowing then what I know now.

Heartless

The queasiness that had lurked in my gut all day gathered itself up in a rocketing wave and launched itself out and onto the pavement. I let it subside then shut my door and started up my car. My lonely heart wanted to stay but I decided to drive away. I drove away from the birthday lunch and away from Dad and his successful new family and away from their pretty scenes and their peaceful hearts. I drove away from the cruel reminder of all that I did not have. I drove and drove, my gut churning and my sobs quaking, until I nearly ran out of petrol in some god-forsaken who knows where.

The petrol station was sun-bleached and wind-wearied, a lonely throwback from the beginnings of the first automobile. The car took five minutes to fill, long enough for me to settle the sobs churning from my chest and dry the tears into streaks on my face. I kept my face down as I went to pay in the rattling old store.

Ciao, bella.

Number two, please.

Here, take this.

I stole a glance up and saw a robust old Italian man, full-cheeked and generous-lipped, waving a tissue at my face. I burst into tears again.

Ah bella, bella, bella. Life, he can be mean, he can be tough.

Thirty-five

I nodded like a bewildered child with a bruised and bloodied knee, blowing raucously into the tissue.

But you know what he never take from you, eh?

I shook my head.

Your beautiful smile, bella.

I snorted.

Oh no, he got that too.

Ah, did he?

And the silly old man, with pudgy belly bouncing and floppy arms flailing, began to tap dance. My mouth dropped and a girlish giggle escaped before I could clamp it shut. He giggled too, the sound whistling through the gaps of his missing teeth, and I was infected with laughter.

Ah, you see, you see . . . your beautiful smile.

I shook my head, still grinning, and paid him. As he handed me back my change, he grasped my hand.

Don't be sad, bella, let it go . . . let your heart dance with a tap like me. Go home to your husband, let him see you smile.

My heart pounds as I drive back to the flat. Her relentless beat is annoyingly painful and I light up a cigarette to remind her that she is not a carefree tap dancer no matter what some old Italian man might say. My smile has long since faded as I turn into my street. Back to the home I have been trying to make with my Rugged Man and the life that is slowly unravelling around us. It does not feel like home. It never really has. Nowhere has felt like home. Most of my life has been spent without a home that I could go to and feel like I truly belonged in. A home that I could go to and feel like I was truly safe. And now, at thirty-five, when I finally should be able to say that I have made my own home, I am, as always, nowhere.

As I write in my diary, I see the old Italian man's smiling face in my mind's eye, saying 'Let it go'. I remember my proud dad and confident stepsister crossing the street hand in hand and I hear, 'Let it go'. I feel the burden of twenty-eight years of wishing it had been another way and I know I need to 'let it go'. I breathe in the four walls of a flat that will never be home and I long to 'let it go'. I really do. I wish so much that I could let it all go. But how? Why did the old man not tell me that? How?

*

An ill wind whistles down this barren desert landscape. The remnants of a long-forgotten village life rise from the ground, crumbling and charred and eerie. I stumble along an old weathered road, my feet burnt from the hot sand, my mouth blistered

Thirty-five

from drought, my body withered and stooped from exhaustion. This road joins up with its own end and I have been walking on it for several days now, round and round, over and over. A baby is crying somewhere on the roadside and I am trying desperately to find her but the wind seems to carry her cries in all directions and the only thing I can do is keep walking and searching, walking and searching, until I finally collapse near a massive decaying cart wheel.

As I surrender to my death, I see a beautiful bright light burning from the centre of the wheel. I feel my dry dusty heart jolt with the hope of seeing Astintina as she was with her wheel spoke beams of light in the finger painting design sensation. As this brightness takes form, my heart begins to buzz, a curious vibration I have never felt before, like a tenor's warm-up humming tone. The shape becomes clearer, emerging out of the light like an angel on high appearing with blessed love to the lowly. Then, like the silvery thread of a gentle song, it whispers to me.

I am your Little Baby Girl.

The shape is suddenly a divine baby deity, the most exquisite little creature I have ever seen, with a sacred heart of pure love that pulses a beacon beat to mine. I am in a whole other luminous universe, lost in the revelation of this newborn realm.

I am your Little Baby Girl.

Then, the child touches me. Seismic waves of shocking light shatter my body, blast my mind and tear open my soul. My heart fills and explodes with a swelling of omnipotent love.

And I sit bolt upright in bed.

I am sweating and shaking, panting and spinning. It is the dead dark middle of night and a dry summer breeze blows in through the bedroom window. My Rugged Man seems to be fighting his own demon nightmares in the dark so my fright has not woken him. I climb out of bed and steal into the kitchen. I switch on the light and it sears my eyes with its strangely comforting glare. I am here, in my very own kitchen, where the cockroaches are feasting on the dirty dinner plates, where the light in the fridge is still not working, where the festering carton of rancid milk still sits alongside the opened carton of fresh milk, where the glasses have not been rinsed properly and still have my lipstick on their rims.

I am here, in the apartment I share with my Rugged Man, close to but not quite a barren desert landscape. I drink down my glass of cold milk, hoping it will stop my stomach from continuing to indulge in its tedious queasiness. I dare not think about the dream. I sit on the balcony and shallow

Thirty-five

breathe in the warm air, trying not to move my rib cage too much. I refuse to think about the dream. I stand over my Rugged Man as he lies in bed and I feel a surge of suppressed hate shudder through my body and a loathing of myself living in everyday fear of his erratic violence and I wonder what it would be like to stab him dead with my steak knife. And still, the dream stays with me.

Finally, I pull out my black shiny diary to exorcise the dream out of my mind and onto the paper and stop this rattling in my soul so I can get back to sleep. Almost immediately, it falls open to an empty page with the heading 'Twenty Things in My Life That Bring Me Joy'.

That damned stupid list.

Four hopeless hours later, lonely and lost, I still have not written one thing. As I watch the sun rise, I see the harsh light of my life's true desolation. I cannot deny it any longer. There is nothing, no thing, not anything, in my life that I can say brings me joy. Nothing. I think I have even forgotten what joy feels like. I think I am even a little scared of it. But most frightening of all, I cannot think of a way to get it.

And there it is again, that old throb of my heart's ache. I have got so used to it, so numb in my chest cavity, the feeling barely register. But it has been there all the time, ready and waiting for an onerous moment of self-reckoning. A deeper ache it is now, with a heavier base, more weight, holding a gloomy pool of sadness within it. And a bitter, gaping emptiness that seems to be intent on sucking all my life force into it like a gigantic, greedy, grisly black hole.

There is not one thing in my life that brings me joy, let alone twenty. That is the undeniable truth. I close my diary.

*

It is a full four weeks later that I finally buy a pregnancy testing kit. The queasiness that has taken up permanent residence in my gut nearly overtakes my whole being at the chemist counter. I tremble with an overwhelming sense that something dreadfully important could be happening. That something irreversibly revolutionary may be about to rise up and overthrow my whole life.

During a lull in the usually busy toilets at work, I hide myself away in the end cubicle. I suck in a deep breath, remove the wrapping as quietly as I can, hold my sucked-in breath and take the pregnancy test. Then wait. The uncertain silence around me is roaring and my fingers quiver holding their questioning future. Slowly, surely, a second blue line appears, like some mystical sign from the cherubic

Thirty-five

being growing in my womb that she is really here, making her mark with an imaginary hand. The quivering in my fingers takes over every fibre in my body. My eyes start to lose their focus as I stare at the proof of her presence. I hear the far-away tinkling of angel bells singing.

She is here. She has come. Behold, your Little Baby Girl.

My resurrecting heart starts to pound an ecstatic, fanatically erratic beat, sending my spinning mind into a nearly uncontrollable spiral. It is all I can do to keep my sanity by silencing her with the vicious thought that I am not sure if I will keep the foetus yet. This shuts her up into a hard little ball of hatred. It also serves to still my mind and sedate my body so I can consider this with crystal clarity. I am pregnant, at thirty-five, in a troubled relationship and a disturbed state of being. Is this really the path I should take?

I carried this question through the day, during the evening and into the night. I could not sleep with this question burning a fever through my body. Is this really the path I should take? Then, just before the sun began his rise, and just after an early bird sang her dawn serenade to the day, my answer came. A tiny tender thud. A soft serene stroke. A pure precious pulse. This was my exquisite answer.

Heartless

The gentle and powerful and pristine and celestial beating of my blessed Little Baby Girl's heart. I could feel it, quietly clear and strong, her sacred heart nestled and beating deep inside me, and it was life-saving succour to my soul. I saw the path undeniably direct and stretched out at my feet. It was her immaculate heart that would guide me now. I had found at last my true Great Life Purpose.

That day, I checked myself into clean and cheap self-contained accommodation in a civilised part of the big city. That night, as my Rugged Man slept, I furtively packed a few favourite things into the only two suitcases I would take as the sum total of my life. Some clothes, my diaries, my trusty steak knife, three old family photographs, a wrapped-up-in-brown-paper poster and a green-and-white-striped shoe box. I stealthily loaded them into the boot of my car. I wrote my Rugged Man a note wishing him well and left him a month's rent in cash. Then, I hopped in my car and let it roll as far down the street as it could by itself. At the last possible minute, I turned the engine on and drove off into the dawn of my next start again.

*

My water broke at the end of a long day in the office. My timing was perfect; it was a Friday, the deadlines

Thirty-five

had been met and the Succubus was appeased. My Little Baby Girl was incredibly considerate. I called Mum and was able to book her on the very next bus to the city. I caught a taxi to the hospital and terrified the old Indian driver with my heavy breathing. I told him not to worry, I was only breathing like this because I had just gone into labour and he very nearly had a head-on collision with a semitrailer.

My Little Baby Girl was keen to arrive and I had a miraculously quick labour. Every part of me was eager to see, to touch, to hold this precious little being in my arms and gaze upon her beautiful newborn heart. For once, I could feel my own ragged heart working alongside me, keeping the blood rich with oxygen and pumping it like a vigilant warrior to everywhere it was needed. Although, at the very end, I did make her promise to hide away so we did not spook the child from the outset with our ugliness.

Finally she arrived, my Little Baby Girl, red and bloody and kicking and screaming, but soul-wrenchingly beautiful. I cradled her tight and close and stroked her with a feeling of the greatest of Great Love and whispered in her ear the solemn promise that I would never ever leave her. As I finally found the courage to look upon her luminous little heart, every cell in my body was charged with an electric light that shone away all the darkness from my soul. From the very core of my being a deep cry was released, of love, of pain, of hope, of fear, of a profound something I could not name. I rocked her in my arms with these overwhelming cries cascading over us both until I finally understood their fundamental nature. Joy.

And for the first time in almost forever, I felt my heart flush with her own exhilarated pain. This cauterising pain of joy.

*

Mum stayed with me for three weeks, teaching me how to change nappies, breastfeed and burp properly, swathe the right way and learn the mysterious art of interpreting baby language so that my Little Baby Girl's cries were not the death of both of us. She helped me baby-proof my modest, two-bedroom, rented apartment with special locks on cupboards and bright-pink plastic fencing and luscious lamb's wool rugs. She bought cuddly toys and jingling mobiles and pop-out picture books. She decorated the baby's bedroom with hanging fairies and night-time lights and pixie printed curtains. Finally, she could indulge her trinket addiction and not feel a whiff of guilt.

During this time, I watched my mother surge with a fresh transfusion of new life. The wrinkles

Thirty-five

of loneliness and creases of pain smoothed out on her face and I wondered how this lovely woman could have been left so far behind. I stood back as she transformed the space into a playful little cave of vibrancy and fun and bit my tongue when she insisted on fixing my finger-painted poster of Astintina in pride of place on the wall overlooking the baby's cot. I silently planned to remove it the minute she left but when my Little Baby Girl first saw the painting she laughed out loud and clapped her hands and danced in my arms and so, Astintina was allowed to stay.

The night of the day Mum left on the bus to go home, I felt the tremendous reality of just the two of us, my baby and me, walking our combined life path alone. As I lay her in her cot and patted her to sleep, I assured her, and myself, all would be well. I promised her I would always take special care of the needs of her delicate heart. That I would always listen closely to her little heart's desires. That I would always follow diligently her exquisite heart's commands. That I would never, ever, break my Little Baby Girl's innocent heart.

And I promised her that even though my own jaded heart is as good as lost and absent and non-existent to the outside world, for her, my Little Baby Girl, and her precious little heart, I will forever be present and available and always at hand. And as she drifted off to sleep, I leaned in close, looked directly at her heart and gave her my eternal vow. That, in spite of my own heart's suicidal ache, for her, my blessed Little Baby Girl, I will never, ever, be heartless.

forty-two

I AM SO EXHAUSTED I cannot move. I am now a weary member of the Working Mother's League of the Walking Dead. Tonight, my body has gone into a stubborn state of paralysis and refuses to shift as little as the inch I need to reach the remote. So I am forced to lay prostrate on the couch and simply stare at the seductively blank television screen, which silently begs me to turn it on. My eyes eventually drift to my Little Baby Girl's extensive collection of dolls and doll paraphernalia that are strewn in various states of undress across the floor in front of me. I gaze at them with a persistent perplexed horror that in spite of my spirited resistance, she still loves to play with them the most. Mercifully, she plays with matchbox cars and plastic building contraptions as well so I can rest a little easier knowing some sort of dynamic equilibrium is being achieved.

The small hand on the clock has only just hit eight and I know it is too disgustingly early for me to crash now. Amidst groans and grimaces and cracks and creaks, I haul myself off the couch, steady my aching body on its fluid-filled feet and follow the trail of playtime debris around the house. I pick up an assortment of miniature cars and plastic spaceships, fairy wings and magic wands, horses' heads with reins on broomsticks, and dump them all in the play trunk. I gather a collection of uplifting books on ugly ducks turning into swans and caterpillars emerging as butterflies, pseudo-exercise DVDs with various dancing bananas and dinosaurs and absurdly dressed humans, CDs featuring a mediocre array of arrangements on the theme 'Bop Till You Drop', and file them all haphazardly in the play library.

As quietly as I can, I creep down the hall to her bedroom and peer in, just for a moment. It seems I am never fully prepared for the scene of breathtaking beauty that greets me. There she sleeps, my Little Baby Girl, all grown up at seven, adorned in pink elfin pyjamas and her favourite cuddly bears, and lost to a sandman world of nourishing slumber. For many years, I would weep when I watched her.

Forty-two

Now, my eyes sting and my throat constricts but I swallow the sob and keep a regular breath. As I reluctantly leave, my eye is caught by the sparkling image of a brilliant white and golden Astintina hanging above my Little Baby Girl's head. It is as if she whispers to me not to worry, that the precious little one is safe under her watch, that she is enveloped in a protective bubble of gentle golden light. And it reassures me, for I feel it is in some way true, and it helps me surrender a smidgeon of my need to latch onto and look over my Little Baby Girl's every living moment.

Sitting on the one comfortable wicker chair that can actually fit on my big-city small back porch, I light one of the few cigarettes I smoke on a regular basis these days. Gone are the long indulgent nights of escapist alcohol and mind-numbing marijuana. While the drive towards self-destruction still exists in my core, I take one look at my Little Baby Girl's pristinely pure heart and vow to never taint it with the troubles of mine and her darker tendencies.

And I think I have done well. I worked hard at the Succubus' feet and slowly climbed up her authority and pay-scale ladder to reach the giddy top. I saved every last penny I could and, in doing so, conquered my addiction to handbags and heels and hordes of accessories. I mothered with all the passion and street smarts I had, insisting a creche be established at work and attitudes be moved into the twenty-first century. I refused the half-hearted social invitations from would-be friends and surrendered, not unhappily, to an austere life of child and television and early nights. And finally, last year, my Little Baby Girl and I were able to move out of our rented apartment and into our very own, modest, semi-attached house.

My very first, very own, home. From the moment we moved in on that magical day we made a sanctuary of love and belonging and safety and certainty. Our creative whims were set free and we painted everything in sight, pulled up the carpet and put nails in the walls wherever we wanted. Whatever my Little Baby Girl's heart desired, we did.

And now, we have moved on to the reformation list for our backyard. First thing of paramount importance is the construction of a tree house in the accommodating old gum, near the soon-to-be Hill's-Hoist-into-swing conversion. The builder has already assembled a rustic ladder and a few planks for the floor and will be back on the weekend to finish the rest. I imagine my Little Baby Girl climbing up there with her special things and imaginary scenes, clinking tea cups and talking to herself, looking out for pirates and gremlins and marauding

Forty-two

armies, all the while radiating with the sheer delight of unfettered fun. That is how I would have been if I had the tree house I always wanted. The old longing stabs my heart more fiercely than I thought it would and I light a second cigarette, like in the old days, just to stop the annoying soreness.

I too will play in my very own dream tree house after all, I write in my new, fake leopard-skin-covered diary.

*

Upon the Succubus' retirement two years ago, I assumed the title and privileges of editor of the magazine. They say power corrupts, and judging by the fleeting whispers that float past me in the common corridors, I have become like the old guard, my very own version of a human Hydra. I understand now how it can happen. Over the years I learnt to raincoat myself against the gossip and questioning and derision that drizzled around me like a dank mist in the magazine hallways. I learnt to relinquish the need to eavesdrop near the staffroom and attempt to adjust my demeanour to appease their catty tongues. I learnt to embrace the qualities they endowed me with and now, the stylish hive of beige and burgundy cubicles that stretch out before my office buzz with my bidding.

Heartless

Today, I have the pleasure of interviewing applicants for the auspicious role I first filled fourteen years ago, General Dogsbody. The scene plays out similar to my memory, although now I am the Succubus sitting behind the desk and I stalk, with my icy eyes, the parade of young, mostly female, hopefuls that pass before me. I wait, as the same endless stream of typically flawless fashionista women trickle through. I detect in their hearts the lusty ambition and potential for betrayal that lurked in the heart of my university best friend, Fiona. I see clearly the covert killer instincts that I observed from a different angle years ago. That feline patience they possess to track and tease their unsuspecting prey for the perfectly timed fatal pounce. And I knew, sooner rather than later, I would be that prey.

Like my cunningly clever, silver-haired and Chanel-suited predecessor, I wait for my galley slave to reveal herself. Before long, she enters, nervous and trembling, clutching for dear life a familiar hotchpotch of a portfolio that holds barely anything of importance within it. Cruelly, I have kept that booby trap of a fat Persian rug and predictably she trips on it. As she falls, she nearly crashes against the corner of my desk and I stand up to help her, without even thinking, out of some maternal instinct of protection, unlike the Succubus, who never had children.

Forty-two

The girl catches herself in time and flashes me this look of hideous embarrassment, which my whole being recognises and understands. My heart stabs a painful memory through my body and I decide to ease her agony with a smile.

Please excuse my lethal rug. It is not long for this world.

Oh, sorry, I, um ... it's really lovely though ... um, really thick.

I spare her the torture the Succubus inflicted on me. I tell her that while her portfolio is thin, it shows some talent. I tell her that the job is a lowly one but it is a step on the ladder and it may lead somewhere. I tell her it is where I started. I tell her I got where I am through hard work and loyalty and that, were she to be the successful applicant, I would expect the same. I do not lacerate her timid heart with the truth that she is the least impressive of the applicants, nor tell her not to harbour any great ambition. I decide I do not want to be the one that extinguishes her grand plans for a Great Life Purpose. Life will no doubt do that anyway.

She leaves, her spirit intact for now. Perhaps I am not cut out for the role of thrashing Hydra after all. Perhaps the memory of my god-forsaken self at that age dulls my desire to inflict similar pain. Either way, whatever the reason, my goodwill has not stopped my vitriolic heart from shooting knife points of pain all around my chest cavity. It takes cool water, three heartburn tablets and ten breaths to calm her down.

*

Yet another long, boozy executive lunch wooing potential pretentious advertising clients, whilst stacking on at least five extra kilos, ruins my Wednesday. Everything is dripping in a creamy sauce or a wine jus or a generous shave of butter. And of course, it is only polite to partake of the odd glass of cabernet sauvignon or two with everyone else. The advertising men's chatter fades into the distance as I scan the menu for a simple dish. I order the veal tenderloin medallions wrapped in fresh sage and prosciutto, pan-roasted and served with white wine, sage, butter and reduced jus on a bed of truffled mash. I wonder what happened to good old sausages and plain old mash. I vow to myself that I will get through this hectic week then start the latest diet fad with real discipline the following Monday. I stare with unrestrained envy at the stunning, Swedish, impossibly stick-thin waitress taking our orders and wonder how she got so lucky. Then I snap back to attention as, predictably, when she leaves, the eyes of the four men at the table follow

Forty-two

her all the way to the kitchen with barely concealed wantonness.

Ranging between the ages of twenty-seven and fifty-three, these four men, without exception or exaggeration, have sized up almost every woman in the restaurant. Those who looked in the thirties bracket were given at the most a courteous glance-over, unless ample cleavage was on display, then the look lingered at said breasts for substantially longer. Any woman under thirty has been subjected to a lengthy physical assessment, with some even warranting quiet conferring among the men and embarrassingly indiscreet nods and smirks in the lady's direction. For the rest of us, those over forty and looking tired and worn and old and past it, not even a cursory glance. Not even a momentary acknowledgement of our actual existence.

That night, as I undress for my empty bed, trying not to think about my older woman unattractiveness and single woman loneliness, another prickling stab punctures my heart. Unsettled, I replay the scenes from lunch and while I feel some relief in knowing I am no longer fair game for the feasting eyes of somewhat predatorial men, there is also a tinge of something else. Perhaps regret, perhaps confusion, perhaps despondency. Not out of some egotistical need to be lusted after, but from that very human need resting within all of us, regardless of age or gender or class or colour, to feel desired and desirable, to feel wanted and valued. To love and be loved.

For some foolish reason, I had honestly thought I had been able to extinguish the yearning for these things years ago, but there it sits still, quiet, unabated. Even though I am now over forty and officially old. And in the image-obsessed society of the moment, which places unimaginable worth on female youth, there is no safe haven for older women, no temple of respect or significance or appreciation, in which to seek some respite. Weary, I write in my diary. There is no country for old women.

Eventually I crawl into my bed, alone, check for my steak knife in my pillowcase and call Mum.

Hey, it's me.

Geez, love, it's late.

Oh, sorry, did I wake you?

No, no . . . just watching the telly.

Oh, good.

Is everything all right?

Yeah, yeah, we're both good.

Oh, now, I've been meaning to ask, is her hair getting too long?

Actually, she could do with her fringe trimmed soon.

Forty-two

Well, you let me know when it's a good time to come down.
You were always good at that.
What?
You always kept my hair trimmed.
Better than paying someone else to do it.
You would've been a good hairdresser.

Mum stays quiet on the other end of the line.

Didn't you want to be a hairdresser?
Oh, maybe, I don't know . . . you came along.
Why didn't you take it up when I went to school?
Oh, you know . . . things change.

I did know. Her husband left her and her life fell out of her hands.

Have you had your own hair done recently, Mum?
Oh, no, it's just too expensive these days.
But you love having it done!
Oh well, you can't have everything.
You can have your bloody hair done! When you come down next, I'm going to take you to get your hair done, all right?
But it's too . . .
All right?
Oh, love . . .
Mum!
Okay, okay.
A girl's got to have her hair done.

Well yes, that would be nice.
Good, done.
Thanks.

When I finally fall asleep, I have another recurring running-in-the-street nightmare, similar to when I was seven. Once again, I am in my pyjamas and I am running down the middle of a very nice street, trying to knock on the front doors of all the lovely-looking houses. Only this time, I am not being chased by anything, although I am still incredibly upset. I clutch in my hand a note, which I desperately need to give to someone in particular. I knock on the first front door, calling out for them to let me in, but no one answers. They are sitting near their front window eating a nice family dinner and they can hear me but will not open their door for me. I race to the next house and get the same response. I grow more and more frantic as I fear my note will not be delivered. But still, no one will let me in. No one will help me. No one cares. At this point, I usually wake up.

But tonight, the dream continues. I finally get to the last house on the street. On display in their front window is a coffin and it seems a funeral wake is taking place. I go to knock on the door but it swings wide open without my touching it. I wander in. No one registers my presence. I am drawn to the open

Forty-two

casket and while something inside me wants to run away, I summon my courage and peer into it. There, looking serene and so very handsome, is my Beautiful Man. My heart stops beating and I fall to the floor. The note drops from my hand and opens. It reads 'Forgive me'.

I wake up in a cold sweat, unable to breathe, unable to move. I cannot feel my heart beating. I panic, thinking I may be dead. Then I hear a soft, sweet little voice in the night.

Mummy? Are you all right?

My Little Baby Girl stands in the doorway, frowning. The vision kick-starts my heart and I laugh.

Sure I am, Sweetpea.
You were making funny wailing noises.
Just having a bad dream.
Can I snuggle up with you?
Yes, please.

And the ghastly dream recedes into the ghostly black of night.

*

It is truly frightening how history repeats itself. It is the week of my Little Baby Girl's all-important, first time ever, dance class performance for the public, called *The Magical Flight of the Twinkle*

Toes Spectacular. She is supposed to be some sort of strange supernatural fairy type and while I have wanted to take her to a fancy-dress costume-hire store to make everyone's life easier, she insists on dressing up as Astintina. Apparently, my mum has been in my Little Baby Girl's ear and described the wondrous outfit in sensationalised detail and now nothing else will do.

Having paid a crotchety local seamstress an exorbitant amount of money to work up some sort of outfit off my finger-painted design, we finally get the costume the night before the Spectacular. It is a virtual replica of my crazy Mysterious Imaginings Number Seven dress, complete with a wheel spoke sun of light beams strapped to the back and a gold foil-wrapped, sparkling love heart in the centre of the chest. When my Little Baby Girl puts it on, I ricochet in time to the backstage mayhem of Miss Blossoms' Magical Wonderland Ride with Alice and Her Mysterious Imaginings. I had just gulped down two cups of strawberry crush cordial and desperately needed to go to the toilet. My heart was panicking and fluttering like a freaked-out butterfly in an unfriendly rib cage, making me feel horribly sick in my stomach. Now, at forty-two, staring at my Little Baby Girl dressed as Astintina, my frightened heart is flapping around all over again.

Forty-two

No matter what I try leading up to the Spectacular, deep breathing, indigestion tablets, heat packs, cool packs, heartburn tablets, lapis lazuli crystals, yoga stretching and, finally, four tablets of hospital-grade pain-killers, my rabid heart will not stop her madness. Sitting in the dance auditorium, alongside a nervous audience of pleased-as-punch parents, I feel faint and breathless and buzzing with an odd and edgy sensation. Like a restlessness, a foreboding, a trapped-in-a-collapsing-building feeling.

Finally, my Little Baby Girl comes out. She is the sweetest, dearest cherub of a creature on the stage, swaying her hips and flapping her arms, completely out of rhythm and time. She almost knocks over a cardboard cut-out of a tree with her wheel spoke beams of light, but she recovers like a true professional and blazes on regardless. In fact, it serves to make her joyous heart radiate even brighter. My Little Baby Girl and her luscious heart dance up a storm, shining and sparkling and glowing and glittering. Together, they are a truly divine sight to behold, innocent and pure and magnificent and magical. They are the absolute elemental meaning of adorable and beautiful and blessed and sacred. I randomly think, with a choking lump in my throat, how could anyone abandon such an angel?

Suddenly, the room is spinning and I am

clutching the chair. A death adder pain is striking through my chest and down my left arm. I am nauseous and dizzy. I can barely take a breath. I cannot feel my legs. More horrifying, I cannot appease the agony writhing through my heart. And I cannot stop the primal cry wailing from my soul, the sobbing of a similar sparkling seven-year-old innocent, how could Dad abandon me? After all these years, having buried itself so deep, this dark, deathly pain has finally raised itself up and launched its fatal attack at my heart.

As I fall to the floor, before everything goes white, the last thing I see is my Little Baby Girl's terrified face.

*

It seems all those clichés have some merit after all. I am flying furiously fast down a tunnel-like vortex, hurtling towards a sphere of light hovering at the end. As I burst out the end of this curving dimension, the white light morphs into a strikingly magnificent woman. She seems to hover in front of me, a smiling face and a glowing body, with a familiar and fiercely powerful energy. She speaks to me, although her mouth does not move and I seem to hear the words with my mind rather than my ears.

Forty-two

You do not recognise me?
Um, are you the Virgin Mary?

She throws back her head and laughs, this time her mouth opening wide.

I'll give you a hint, I have no arms or feet.

Suddenly, an electric ray of light shoots out from her chest and pierces mine, searching for my heart, which has disappeared somewhere, and it strikes me who she is.

Astintina?
Yes.
But you were a figment of my imagination.
No. I am your soul.

I thud back into my body. Sirens wail all around me and I am being hoisted into the back of an ambulance. I see the tear-streaked, ashen-white face of my Little Baby Girl being comforted by a female paramedic. I try to call out to her, to tell her not to worry, to tell her I will not break my promise, I will not leave her, but I cannot speak. All I can do is raise my right hand out towards her. She sees it and breaks free from the carer's embrace, screaming.

Mummy!

I hurtle again through unknown planes of mysterious consciousness to slam into a seat next to Astintina. We rest on cushions of light, angled so that we look up to an iridescent, other-worldly cinema screen. Images from my life flash an unsettling montage, enormous and confronting, on the massive screen.

I need to get back to my Little Baby Girl!
Watch.
No! I must be with her. I am not meant to be here!
Yes you are.

And with a wave of her hand, Astintina pauses the reel on a still frame of me at thirty-five, patting my tiny newborn Little Baby Girl to sleep.

This is a beautiful scene. A mother pledges her unconditional love to her blessed baby. She promises to always obey this little one's precious and pure heart. But what of her own heart?

Then Astintina moves to the next series of frames. It is much earlier that same year. I sit, red-faced and sweating, rugged up in my cardigan on a hot summer's day, vomiting on the pavement, as my dad walks my twenty-one-year-old baby stepsister into lunch. Then, writhing in bitter rejection, I drive away. Astintina gazes steadily at me.

But did your lonely heart not want to try and belong?
I need to get back to my child!
You must watch.

The next scene is ugly and I do not care to watch

Forty-two

it. My cut lip, my swollen face, my Rugged Man cradling me claustrophobically, begging my forgiveness. I stand to go. Astintina smiles with painful sympathy.

This is the truth of your life. You must see and understand.

And so I watch the scene where I acquiesce, in some sort of shameful understanding and masochistic self-loathing, to a life of fluctuating violence and possessive love, having given my promise to stay with my Rugged Man.

Still more painful scenes follow. Astintina shows me at the interview with the Succubus. I watch as I allow my undernourished spirit to be decimated and my fragile, tucked-away dreams to be destroyed on the vicious whim of an unfulfilled and mean-spirited woman. Further back in time, I see myself, drunk and stoned, kneeling in front of my Rugged Man. I watch as I see the truth of his damaged heart and know it could never really love me and yet I decide to give myself to him regardless.

Then, Astintina holds my hand and gives it a reassuring squeeze, as she shows me the scene where I give back my Beautiful Man's heart. I watch myself tell this extraordinary man that his magnificent heart was not for me. That our hearts would never get along. That he was wrong in his judgment when he thought his heart was meant for me. That he should take his heart back and leave. I watch as his breathtakingly beautiful heart breaks into two and he places it back into his body. I am sobbing now. Astintina shakes her head sadly.

You denied both of your hearts true love that day.

Please, no more.

But this is how it was.

Again, I am forced to watch more awful scenes from my adolescent years. In a swelling sea of nausea, I watch myself being raped by my boyfriend's friend at the party I snuck out to. It makes me want to scream and rage and howl and roar at the terrible pain of it all. Then, I see myself at the interstate bus stop, months earlier, during school holidays, holding my dad tight before I have to leave. I watch as I glance over with envy at his new family and it makes me stop myself from telling him I love him. Still further back in time, I see the scene at the oval behind the netball courts. Although it was not really what I wanted, I watch as I give my virginity to a boy because he tells me he loves me.

I want to get back to my Little Baby Girl!

Astintina shushes me, then speaks in a hushed and reverent tone.

There is one more scene you need to see. It is the key, the cause, the catalyst for all these events, these choices

Forty-two

you have made. You will see the very reason why you decided to tread this path.

And she plays me the moments after Dad left. I watch myself, as a frightened little girl of seven, kneel down to collect my broken, bruised and bleeding heart. She has been kicked into a dirty and dusty corner, with pieces missing, and she is scared to look at me. I do not want to look at her either, blaming her for everything that happened. I watch as I put her back into my chest and promise myself that I will never look at or listen to her again. Astintina turns to me.

And you kept your promise. You have never looked at or listened to your heart since that time. You have ignored her desires, her aches, her warnings. You assumed she was ugly and battered and blackened, so you chose not to follow her when you should have. And these life scenes you have just reviewed are the consequence. Is it any wonder you have had this attack of the heart?

Thud! I am back in my body again. I frantically search for my heart, but I cannot find her. Fluorescent lights and nurses' faces flash frantically in front of me and I get hit with that loathsome big-city hospital smell. I can feel the fear clustered in the corridors and I try not to let it climb on and choke me. The trolley I cling to slams through a set of swinging doors, jolting me upright and, as the doors reverberate closed, I see in the cracks my Little Baby Girl standing shocked and forlorn, unutterably alone.

I shout at Astintina.

I will not die! I will not leave her!

But you have no Great Life Purpose! You have said it yourself, over and over. So why live?

SHE is my Great Life Purpose!

Really? You really want that precious little one to carry such a heavy burden? To be responsible for providing you with your Great Life Purpose?

Well, no . . . not when you put it like that.

I would hope not.

But I promised I would not leave her!

Suddenly, the luminous white sky starts raining down an eclectic collection of books. As they drop to the ground in a surprisingly neat line, I see they are beginning to look suspiciously like my earthly diaries. I spot my childhood favourite, pink-with-purple-dots-coloured diary beside the space-themed, black-with-blue-planets diary from my teens. There lies my white regulation uni student diary next to the soft leather, faded burgundy writing book clasped closed by a delicate bronze butterfly, given to me by my Beautiful Man's sister. How fortunes changed, as evidenced by the next,

Forty-two

no-frills, plain Jane, supermarket-bought diary. Then, my Rugged Man gave me the hard-covered and crisp, coloured-with-roses diary as a house-warming present. Coming later, my shiny black recycled paper diary, and last of all my current, fake leopard-skin-covered diary.

Astintina's eyes shine as she surveys the battered diaries.

Here, in these books, you had your Great Life Purpose.

What do you mean?

Not bodice rippers or Atlantis adventures or futuristic science-fiction fantasies. You didn't finish them because they meant nothing to you.

But those stories were all I had.

You're mistaken. These books were the keys to what you were meant to do.

Write about myself?

Much more than that. Write from your heart.

I look at the gaping hole in my chest.

She has left me.

Ah, she has finally granted you your wish.

What wish?

To be heartless.

A revelatory bolt of white lightning strikes me blind for an instant. As my sight recovers, I see bright surgical lights blaring at me from above. I feel an oxygen mask on my face and tubes going in and out of my body. Then, I see Astintina, as she appeared to me as a child. Fairy-small and radiantly golden. A shaft of brilliant light streams from the centre of her chest and rather than the beam connecting with mine, it seems to hold something just out of my reach for me to look upon. As my eyes adjust to the light, I see it is my very own heart. I tremble at the sight of her for, it is true, I have not looked at her for thirty-five years. I expect her to be scarred and mutilated, black and ugly, small and shrivelled. Instead, she is big and loud and red and dancing. As she was when I was seven. As she always has been.

Then, Astintina sings to me, in a ritualistic tone that speaks of last rites.

Here is your heart. Do you agree that you have denied your heart her true desires?

Yes.

Do you agree that you have long wished to be heartless?

Yes.

Is it your choice now to continue to ignore your heart's existence?

No!

Astintina pauses, bemused.

No?

Forty-two

No.

Then what do you wish for your heart to do?

To come back to me.

I see.

And to forgive me.

Ah ... but your heart wants to know if you can forgive yourself?

After a long moment, I whisper my glorious epiphany.

Yes.

Slowly, my beautiful heart descends into my chest. The reunion infuses every part of my being with brilliant white light. I am lost in her, immersed in her, enjoined with her. I surrender entirely to this final joyous ecstasy.

And I feel my heart beat once again.

*

Far off in the distance, I hear the twittering of tiny birds making a nest. Or is a radio somewhere twirling out a tinny pop song? I try to tune in my ears. The sound becomes more like the high-pitched whisper of a woman nearby. Then suddenly, another sound, deep, sonorous, commanding but gentle, resonates clearly in my ear. It sounds very close by and vaguely familiar. I struggle to open my eyes. They are leaden heavy and sticky with sleep. I just manage to prise them open a few millimetres with my mind. All I see is a cloudy blur with some hazy movement that seems to hover above me. I will my eyes to focus and slowly a picture becomes clearer.

What I see is beyond belief. It is clear that I have died. For leaning over me, in a white stiff-collared shirt, emanating tender concern, is my Beautiful Man. I gasp.

Am I in heaven?

Definitely not.

He laughs, warm and mellow, and I see that he is older now. Time has creased a furrow between his eyebrows and lines laugh out from his eyes. His mouth is as generous as ever, but his cheeks are more sallow, as if life has sucked the youthful plumpness from them. His hair is thinner now and it wears its greying hues with dignity and a little pride. A quality of well-travelled wisdom animates his features now, speaking of a vast spectrum of varied experience and an assured strength of character that has carried him safely through. I steal a quick glance to his sleeve but it is bare. He does not seem to wear the projection of his heart there anymore.

You might like to know, I carry this everywhere, as my lucky charm. And I certainly think it helped us keep you alive last night.

Forty-two

And he pulls from his pocket, placing it on the pad of his fingertip where it fits perfectly, the small but flawless, pure, rose-gold love heart I gave him for Christmas, twenty-one years ago.

I'll leave you with your family now.

And he points to the corner of the room where my mum and my Little Baby Girl are waiting. I burst into tears.

They rush over to me with their own tears flowing and their arms yearning for hugs and, as we embrace and sob and sniffle and laugh, my Beautiful Man slips away.

*

Mum has been an extraordinary help, staying with me, catering to my every need and looking after my Little Baby Girl, while my heart and I have slowly rehabilitated. Tonight, she is helping me prepare a very special dinner and stirs the soup while I get ready. I have decided to wear a simple but, hopefully, elegant, long black dress, with my hair up and just a hint of make-up. As I look at myself in the mirror, my excited heart starts jumping up and down, singing to me that the timing is right. Her excitement is infectious and, with total trust in her judgment, I go to my wardrobe and pull out my cherished green-and-white-striped shoe box.

As I gaze at the treasures inside, my heart is racing with so much delight my hands start to shake. First, I take out the painfully adorable, raggedly little rascal of a teddy bear with scruffed-up ears and sink-into-me eyes. He looks at me with a profound stare that seems to say 'At last', as I sit him in pride of place on my bed. Next, I unravel the silver pendant bearing the turquoise gemstone of stunning beauty. For the first time ever, I lace it, fingers trembling, around my neck and hope that it will indeed provide the healing I need to fully embrace and express myself tonight.

Then, finally, after so very many years, I open the glimmering gold trinket box that has always sat in the corner of this shoe box. I cannot help but gasp when I open the lid and see the magical contents inside. There it is. The enchanting fairytale of a golden charm bracelet, adorned with alchemical trinkets of suns and moons and stars and magic, given to me at a Christmas long ago by my Beautiful Man. My eager heart flutters in anticipation and my eyes well up with a bittersweet mixture of hope and regret. I lightly touch it and an electric current of love shoots along my agitated nerves, serenading them, appeasing them. I pick it up, feel its golden weight and gentle delicacy, and I hold it tenderly in my hands. It seems to grow even more beautiful.

Forty-two

Finally, I put it on my wrist. It fits perfectly. It tells me it is home at last.

Everything is set and ready to go. It is fifteen minutes before eight, before my guest is due to arrive. Mum has left to go to the movies and my Little Baby Girl is fast asleep. I flit around here and there, adjusting fork positions, refolding napkins, rearranging flowers, stirring the soup, checking on the roast, until my exasperated heart orders me to sit down and relax. So I do. But the minutes tick by in painstakingly slow motion and my mind starts to bubble with thoughts of doom and dread and dark fears. What if he comes and hates the food? What if he comes and we have nothing to say? What if he comes and berates me for breaking his heart? Or worse, what if he decides not to come at all?

With this, my upset heart pounds a scolding beat through my body and a blinding light flashes in front of my eyes. It is Astintina, gently telling my mind to stop its senseless spinning and to trust that everything is as it should be. The doorbell rings. He is five minutes early! I open the door to my Beautiful Man, standing there, more handsome than ever, and I am suddenly in that hospital back alley again, seeing him for the first time and thinking I would dearly love him to be mine.

Sorry I'm early.

No, thank you . . . I was just sitting here, worrying you wouldn't come at all.

He laughs, I melt.

Where's your little girl?

She's asleep already.

She is a gorgeous little spirit.

Yes, she is.

The evening flows smoothly and naturally. He helps me serve dinner and compliments the food and asks after my mother and speaks of his own family and tells me about his work and is curious about mine. The night is nearly over.

That pendant looks lovely on you.

Thank you.

And the bracelet seems to fit nicely.

Perfectly. You chose very well.

Good.

Thank you once again for . . . well, saving my life.

I'm pleased I could. That you wanted to live. There were moments during the surgery I thought we had lost you.

A hush of silence. Then, I ask, tentatively:

You must see a lot of hearts?

Quite literally, hundreds.

How does mine compare?

She is beautiful . . . like I always knew she would be.

Forty-two

And how is your heart?

Ah . . . he keeps himself very busy. He is passionately into our work. Has been since I knew you. It is his drive that has got me to where I am now.

And love?

Well, like I said, my heart has been into our work . . . he has never really been into any periodic romance.

Even ours?

Because of ours.

Suddenly, he takes out his heart and holds it towards me. Again, it is a breathtaking vision. It has lost none of its power, its beauty, its radiance. It still pounds out with vigour and delight an enthralling beat all its own, holding within it a natural strength of greatness in character. It still shines with a compelling enthusiasm, enticing all around it to open to gilded realms where dreams come true. It still pulses with robust health, its colours and hues vibrant with sheer vitality. But, cutting down the very centre of this wondrous heart, is a long, mended, fissure-like scar, a testament to the place where it had broken clean in two, twenty-one years ago.

He is as stunningly beautiful as I remember.
Then why did you not want him?

His carefully casual tone belies the deep and enduring hurt my rejection caused so long ago. I choke on my words.

I wanted him so much. But I knew that if I took your heart, I would have to give you mine in return. And I was ashamed of her.

But she is beautiful.

At the time, and for a very long time both before and after that, I believed she was ugly and deformed and nowhere near worthy of your heart. I thought you would look at her and she would scare you and you would hate me and run away.

And now?

We are at peace with each other.

So, if you had your time again, and we were twenty-one, would you keep my heart?

And cherish him and adore him and respect him and love him forever.

Would you show me your heart now?

Holding my breath, I reach in and pull my heart into the light. She is a little nervous but pulses with a glowing celestial light. When she sees my Beautiful Man's heart on the table, she begins to dance with joy. She dances for him, spinning and twisting and shimmying and twirling. She dances with seduction, with rapture, with the pure ecstasy of being so close to this magnificent heart. And my Beautiful Man's heart watches her with adoration. He shines so bright with a compassion and genuine admiration for this lovely dancing heart. He begins to move with her rhythm, swaying and pulsing, becoming totally lost in her dance of love. My Beautiful Man and I watch them in a shy sort of wonder. Then, he turns to me, eyes sparkling, an enchantingly cheeky smile on his face.

You see . . . I was right. They were meant for each other.

*

Sometimes, it feels like I really did die and am now in heaven. Laying in bed beside my peacefully sleeping Beautiful Man, with my gorgeous Little Baby Girl, serene and cherubic in her bed next door and my trusty old steak knife out from my pillowcase and back in the drawer where it always belonged, everything is so incredibly right with the world. In the still, potent possibilities of this night, I watch our irretrievably-in-love, young-again hearts beat in perfect harmonious time together, a seamless fit, pulsing as one. They both radiate the same brilliant light which seeps into our souls and ignites our bodies and my Beautiful Man and I feel twenty-one again, the dark past barely a fleeting memory as we look upon the new wide world at our feet.

Yes, I am in heaven.

And I am so very thankful that I am here, alive,

Heartless

with my Beautiful Man and our heavenly hearts and that I am not, after all, as I once vehemently wished to be, heartless.

forty-nine

It is 11:32 in the morning when I get the phone call. Dad has been admitted to hospital, here in the big city, with morbidly advanced, terminal lung cancer. He does not have long to live.

I arrive at his hospital room less than an hour later and my knees give way a little when I first see him. He looks so old. While I have spoken to him irregularly on the phone over the past several years, I have not seen him and been privy to the slow visual transformation Time has visited upon him. The most striking memory I have of Dad is being wrapped up in his big strong arms, feeling the force of his frenzied heart pounding out a righteous beat, in battle mode and wielding a metal shield, in the moments before he left. He was not yet thirty then, robust and determined and full of vigour. Now, he is over seventy. The weight of his experience has worn him down and he is much smaller in stature. A reluctant frailty has seeped through his demeanour and his body has begun a begrudging surrender to the inexorable end of its life.

I am not sure what to expect from him, what state the cancer has forced him into. Whether he will be present and lucid or lost entirely to another realm. Whether he will be in unbearable agony or a morphine-induced euphoria. Whether he will even be able to recognise me. But then, as I move closer to his bed, he sees me and his eyes light up and he pats the bed and he struggles to raise himself up. I rush over to help him and together we shift him into a position that faces me.

The exertion leaves him breathless for a while and I can see that he is indeed in a tremendous amount of pain, which he pushes through to engage with me. I see in his eyes an urgency and I feel the atmosphere in the room shift. It is like the meeting of the two of us, alone together, for the first time in a very long time, has charged the air in the room with a weighted reverence, a sense of especial importance. I feel my longing heart grow solemn and still with the hopeful realisation that a true connection with my dad may be about to occur, as I had always wished for, after all this time.

Forty-nine

He touches my arm, I clasp his hand. Tears well up in both of our eyes with complete spontaneous synchronicity.

Hello love.

Hello Dad.

Not long now.

I wouldn't count on it . . . you'll probably kick on forever.

I'm glad you could come.

Of course, Dad, of course.

He regains his breath. He asks me:

Are you happy?

I am now, very happy.

But not always.

Not always, no. Life has had its ups and downs.

He clutches my hand tight and his voice trembles.

I'm sorry I didn't come to your graduation.

Oh Dad, don't worry about it.

I'm sorry I missed so many important things in your life.

Dad, please.

I'm sorry it's taken me so long to tell you.

Dad—

The lump in my throat is choking me as I struggle to hold it down. His eyes are red and watering.

You were such a shining little girl, you know?

Dad—
With such a happy and heavenly heart.
Please—
And I know what me leaving did to you.
Dad—
I know that I broke your precious little heart.

We are both weeping now. It streams out quiet, deep, profound.

I am so sorry—
It's okay—
So very sorry—
It's okay—
My darling little girl.
Dad—
I love you.

I cannot stifle the sobs any longer. I cannot hide what those words stir up in me. I cannot hide how much they mean to me. I cannot hide how much I have longed to hear him tell me he loves me. How I have yearned, how I have raged, how I have wished, how I have begged. How I would have given absolutely anything to have him every day in my life, to have him see me grow, to have him applaud me in the light, to have him hold me close and safe in the dark, to have him kiss me on the head and say 'I love you' and for me to be able to say it back.

Now, forty-two years later, I grasp his hand and

kiss it and rest my head upon it and hold it against my heart and catch my breath and look him directly in his weeping eyes. I tell him.

I love you too.

Exactly seven hours later, at 6:32 in the evening, my father died.

*

I sit on the absolute edge of my all-time favourite, resplendent set of jagged, dramatic big-city cliffs. The magnificent ocean thunders and booms, rumbles and growls as always underneath me. It thrusts its showers of salty spray through the air around me, cleansing me, reviving me, restoring me. I have been sitting here for almost four hours, staring down at the tumultuous thrashing below and out at the serene horizon in front.

People passing by must wonder what that strange old lady, dressed up in a fancy skirt, tailored jacket and shining silver heels, is doing sitting so still, staring at the ocean. Will she fall? Will she jump? Will she walk away? I, too, wonder why I did not change out of my smart new clothes and into something far more suitable for cold cliff sitting. I had just accepted an unexpected writing award for my new book and had made an impromptu speech about my father and it had moved me more than

Heartless

I thought it would so I came straight here to calm myself down, I guess.

The new book is called *Twenty Things That Bring Me Joy*: a good artist is a good thief. I proudly added my thirty-seventh item to my list last week, marvelling that I never would have believed I could experience such joy. My bold-as-brass heart says she always knew but I was too stubborn and scared to listen to her. Astintina insists she was always trying to get me to listen as well, hijacking my dreams whenever she could. I say at least we are back on track now, forging ahead on the path of our Great Life Purpose, with our Beautiful Man and Little Baby Girl beside us. This wonderful reality makes Astintina shine even brighter and my heart dance with passionate pleasure. I too smile with a deep contentment, knowing that I have finally found true healing and forgiveness and safety and belonging. That I am completely loved and love completely in return. I get up to go Home. But not before writing the first line of my next story in my new, covered-in-love-hearts diary.

I have a big, loud, red, dancing heart.

acknowledgements

I would like to thank Madonna Duffy for her generous support and belief, Christina Pagliaro for her hard work and editing prowess, and all those involved on this project at UQP; my wonderful family, Liz, Ray, Jode, Bean and Teegs; my missy moo Kali; and my very own beautiful man, Rove.

THE CHINA GARDEN
Kristina Olsson

Over two hot weeks one summer, cracks emerge in the veneer of a small coastal town.

When a newborn baby is found abandoned in a backyard, this dramatic event pierces the lives of three very different women. Laura has returned home for her mother's funeral after years in exile, only to discover her upbringing was based on a lie. Elderly Cress, who is the moral compass of the community, conceals her own vices, while young Abby walks the streets, her bruises wrapped in baggy clothes. But it is gentle Kieran, an unlikely guardian, who knows their secrets and watches over them.

As their lives collide, what is buried can no longer remain hidden. *The China Garden* is a captivating story about betrayal and its echoes across generations.

'Olsson is a gifted writer with considerable verbal flair . . . a vivid and dramatic novel of small-town secrets.'

Age

'*The China Garden* makes a lovely literary read, particularly for someone who has the time and inclination to set aside an afternoon or two to loll in the sunshine and really immerse themselves in the small town's secrets.'

Bookseller + Publisher

ISBN 978 0 7022 3697 6

UQP

THE DIAMOND ANCHOR
Jennifer Mills

Some secrets take a lifetime to tell.

An unexpected letter from her childhood friend Grace forces May to relive their extraordinary past and confront the events that drove them apart fifty years earlier.

May's father won the Diamond Anchor, a dilapidated pub perched on the ocean's edge, in a game of cards – a gamble which positioned her at the heart of the close-knit community for seventy years, and gave her custody of its stories. Now, trying to maintain a careful balance between the demands of the collapsing building and her own solitary life, May must decide whether to reach out to Grace, whose health is fading, or let her go.

With all the humour and storytelling of small-town life, *The Diamond Anchor* is a brilliant tale of the places and relationships that define us.

Jennifer Mills' awards successes include the Marion Eldridge Award, the Northern Territory Literary Award and the Commonwealth Short Story Competition (Pacific region).

> 'Deftly, sympathetically and with a wry sureness of tone, [Mills] delineates locale, evokes scenery, conjures a community so real its members come and go like familiars, and captures with relish the idiosyncratic speech rhythms of each one of them.'
>
> *Weekend Australian*

ISBN 978 0 7022 3695 2

UQP

THE ANATOMY OF WINGS
Karen Foxlee

- **Winner 2008 Commonwealth Writers' Prize – Best First Book South East Asia and Pacific Region**
- **Winner of the Dobbie Award**
- **Shortlisted for the Barbara Jefferis Award**

Ten-year-old Jennifer Day lives in a small mining town full of secrets. Trying to make sense of the sudden death of her teenage sister Beth, she looks to the adult world around her for answers.

As she recounts the final months of Beth's life, Jennifer sifts through the lies and the truth, but what she finds are mysteries, miracles and more questions. Was Beth's death an accident? Why couldn't Jennifer – or anyone else – save her?

Through Jennifer's eyes, we see one girl's failure to cross the threshold into adulthood. We see a family slowly falling apart. In this award-winning novel, Karen Foxlee captures perfectly the essence of growing up in a small town and the complexities and absurdities of family life.

'An exceptional novel.'

Sydney Morning Herald

'The metaphors embedded in the story and the luscious prose will hold readers until the moving conclusion.'

Publishers Weekly

ISBN 978 0 7022 3698 3

UQP